# Summer Road Trip

## Shooting Lights

### BY MARY VICTORIA JOHNSON

**EPIC Escape**

An Imprint of EPIC Press
abdopublishing.com

# Shooting Lights
## Summer Road Trip

Written by Mary Victoria Johnson

Copyright © 2018 by Abdo Consulting Group, Inc.

Published by EPIC Press™
PO Box 398166
Minneapolis, MN 55439

Printed in the United States of America.

Cover design by Christina Doffing
Images for cover art obtained from iStock
Edited by Rue Moran

LIBRARY OF CONGRESS CATALOGING-IN-PUBLICATION DATA
Names: Johnson, Mary Victoria, author.
Title: Shooting lights/ by Mary Victoria Johnson
Description: Minneapolis, MN : EPIC Press, 2018 | Series: Summer road trip
Summary: Tree has always been content with her quiet village life. It's her best friend,
    Jeanne, who keeps dragging her into trouble. When Jeanne "kidnaps" Tree in order to visit
    Stonehenge for the 1987 summer solstice, their paths tangle with two displaced army kids,
    and what starts out as a simple road trip quickly turns into something far more complicated.
Identifiers: LCCN 2016962617 | ISBN 9781680767254 (lib. bdg.)
    | ISBN 9781680767810 (ebook)
Subjects: LCSH: Adventure stories—Fiction. | Travel—Fiction.
    | Runaway teenagers—Fiction. | Stonehenge (England)—Fiction | Young adult fiction.
Classification: DDC [FIC]—dc23
LC record available at http://lccn.loc.gov/2016962617

*For Mum,*
*for the historical (yikes, sorry!) research help,*
*endless support, and generally being*
*an unstoppable inspiration*

# Chapter One

"GET IN, GET IN!" JEANNE SCREECHED, COMING TO a sudden stop beside me and gesturing wildly. "Hurry, hurry!"

I hopped into the back seat, barely having time to shut the door before we sped off again. "Where's the body?" I asked.

"Already taken care of," Jeanne said, not skipping a beat, "but we gotta hightail it to the airport before Mum looks under my bed."

Judging by the speeds Jeanne was forcing her '67 Morris Traveler to reach, I wouldn't have been surprised if she really was involved with murder.

She kept flicking nervous glances at me through the rearview mirror, muttering a mixture of curses and unintelligible words under her breath.

Used to such behavior and deciding to just go with whatever mad scheme she'd cooked up now, I turned to the window and gazed out at the countryside speeding past us. Typical of Norfolk, there was nothing but fields in every direction, a patchwork of russet and emerald green, littered with the odd clump of trees or the crumbling remnants of a stone wall. Castle Acre village, where I was from, had a population of only a few hundred, and the roads were typically empty. I couldn't think who—or what—Jeanne was trying to get away from.

It wasn't until we whizzed past her farmhouse, a good few miles outside the village, that an inkling of concern crept into my mind.

"Come on then," I said, leaning forward and tapping her on the shoulder. "What's this about?"

She ran her tongue across her lower lip, smearing

lipstick as she did so. "Sit down, Tree. You're going to cause an accident."

To prove that point, Jeanne took a corner at such speed my head smacked against the door . . . and a suspicious shuffling sound resulted from the boot.

"Oi, out of my stuff!" she shouted, still watching me in the rearview mirror as I turned to have a look.

Suitcases. One of them was mine, the name *Teresa Swanson* scrawled across the front in black felt-tip. *Jeanne Wens* and *Random Junk* were thrown in beside it. All three cases appeared stuffed to the brim, their zippers bursting along the seams.

"What the heck?" I exclaimed, properly perturbed now. "Suitcases?"

There was a pause. Then, without a hint of guilt, Jeanne attempted a wink and said, "I'm kidnapping you. Surprise."

Really, it wasn't much of a surprise at all. Being best friends with Jeanne Wens was an occupational hazard, and it wasn't the first time something like this had happened. Instance number one took place mere minutes after we'd first met.

Hailing from Cardiff, Jeanne moved to Norfolk after her parents inherited a property just outside the village. She was cool without trying, probably helped in part by being an upper-middle-class stranger with a different accent in a village that hadn't seen real change since its namesake castle was ruined hundreds of years ago. I, comparatively, was nothing more than another born-and-bred Castle Acre bumpkin. There was absolutely no reason whatsoever she should have picked me out at school, yet pick me out she did.

*"Ever been to McDonald's? Yes, you. Shorty with the big hair. Ever been?"*

I remember shaking my head, trying not to stare. Next thing I knew, we were sitting in the new restaurant munching on the most delicious chips I'd ever tasted, and Jeanne was cheerfully telling me she had no money so she sure hoped I did. But that was how it worked with Jeanne; she'd bring the adventure, and I had to deal with the more practical details.

"I hope this is a temporary kidnapping," I said. "Some of us have jobs now school's done."

Jeanne winked at me. "Sorted. Apparently I sound like your mother—or at least your boss thought so when I phoned you in sick."

I maintained my scowl as I wound down the window, letting a manure-scented breeze filter in. "You gonna pay my lost wages, then?"

One hand on the wheel, she reached into her glove box and threw a handful of loose change at me.

"I hate you," I muttered, pocketing the change all the same.

Jeanne had slowed down now we were properly clear of town. Starship's "Nothing's Gonna Stop Us Now" warbled from the cassette player she'd wedged in the passenger seat, and I found myself humming along like we were simply out for a joyride. Almost reluctantly, after several more minutes, I asked, "So where are we going? Seaside? Club?"

Jeanne's thumb was tapping the wheel in time to the beat. "Stonehenge, actually."

I thought perhaps I'd misheard. "You what?"

"Stonehenge. Remember, the really old rocks that all the tourists—"

"Yeah yeah, but why are *we* going there?"

Jeanne grinned widely. "The summer solstice is in three days, Tree. We're going to see the summer solstice at Stonehenge."

My face fell into my hands. "This is more of your hippie rubbish, isn't it? Genie, you can't keep doing this to me. First Greenham Common, then that weird concert, now *Stonehenge*? Do my parents know?"

Her face fell. "Sure they do. And for the record . . . "

She launched into a rant about how awesome it was going to be and how thankful I should be that she was helping me push my boundaries, and how maybe that concert was a disaster but this wouldn't be, et cetera, et cetera.

Now, Jeanne was the embodiment of everything I aspired to be. She wasn't attractive in the conventional way, with a plain face characterized by an unfortunately crooked nose and a gap-toothed smile, but she carried herself with a surety that seemed to convince everyone—especially the boys—that she was, without question, beautiful. She was tall and long-legged, always dressing to the nines in clothes that emphasized every curve and owning her body with a fierce pride. Red lipstick and bold, perfect eye-makeup, confident and charismatic . . . yet the irony was that Jeanne wanted to be something else entirely. She'd recently traded her jeans for flowy skirts, her band T-shirts for peasant blouses, and let her hair grow out into natural waves. Posters of pop stars were replaced with Greenpeace slogans, and her square-wheeled Allegro was replaced with a barely functional Morris Traveler.

Don't get me wrong, I had nothing against all that folksy stuff. What irritated me was how hard Jeanne was trying to be something she obviously wasn't, when she was so very good at being herself. It was something I'd never brought up, but if I had to take a guess, it was all a backlash against the normalcy of her small-town life. She didn't want to conform; she wanted to stand out, and this was her way of ensuring she did.

"Fine," I said wearily, "go celebrate the solstice. Just drop me off at home first."

She gaped at me like I'd suggested we drown a litter of kittens. "Nuh-uh, Tree, you have to come with me! Road trips are no fun alone." She shook her head forlornly to emphasize her point. "No fun at all. Come on, please? Pretty, pretty please?"

My head began to pound, throwing itself behind Team Go-Home with vengeance. My country roots reviled the idea of large crowds, and I could only imagine how packed Stonehenge would be in three days' time. Jeanne's driving was subpar at best—she'd received her license less than a month ago, after failing four times before—and it was a fifty-fifty shot whether or not her car would make it without falling to bits. Knowing Jeanne, the suitcases in the back were stuffed with everything except what we actually needed, and she probably had no idea where she was going . . .

"Actually," Jeanne said, "I forgot this was an abduction. And you, as the abductee, have no say in the matter."

I groaned. "Do I ever?"

"Rarely," she agreed.

I turned my attention to the window again. We'd entered another village, a collection of flint cottages and red-bricked new builds that mimicked the exact type of houses you'd find in Castle Acre. It was the type of scenery I'd grown up with. In fact, come to think of it, the farthest I'd ever strayed from this area was a school trip to London in primary school. Stonehenge was practically on another planet in comparison.

"Whoops," Jeanne winced, reaching over a manicured nail to turn the cassette player off as it began making strange noises. "I think I forgot to bring more—"

"—batteries?" I suggested, pulling a new pack out of my handbag. "I always keep some for an emergency."

"And this is definitely an emergency." She laughed. "See, Tree, I need you. Think of how bad you'll feel if you abandon me and I never return." She laid a hand across her forehead in mock distress. "Imagine the headlines! 'Gorgeous Eighteen-Year-Old Perishes after Best Friend Bails out of Road Trip: Authorities Believe a Lack of Common Sense Was Involved.'"

Despite myself, I laughed too. "Sounds pretty likely."

"So you're okay with it? Stonehenge Solstice '87?" asked Jeanne, hopefully.

I rolled my eyes and focused on the window. "Fine."

Jeanne whooped, nearly straying onto the wrong side of the road and head-butting an oncoming lorry. Then, like it had never happened, she began chattering on about all the things we were going to do and, again, how fantastic it would all be.

I zoned out, writing a mental diary entry:

*June 18th, 1987. Weather, a balmy twenty-one degrees and mostly clear.*

*My name is Teresa—but you can call me Tree—and I think I'm being kidnapped. I say* think *because I'm not sure if it counts when the kidnapper is your best friend and you know exactly where she's taking you . . .*

# Chapter Two

ALTHOUGH I GAVE IN TO JEANNE'S PLAN, I MANAGED to convince her that taping five hours of *Top of the Pops* didn't count as preparation and we needed to stop and properly plot our route. We stopped in Swaffham, a nearby market town, purchased a motorway map from the newsagent's, and sat down under a rotunda in the square.

"Two nights, I'm thinking," Jeanne said, popping a sweet into her mouth and looking anywhere but the map. "I've got five pairs of undies, anyway."

I glanced at her car, parked in front of an antique shop a little way away. It was cream colored with garish wooden accents around the rear and back wheels. Getting on to be twenty years old, the exterior was remarkably polished, but in terms of functionality, it could barely make it to the next village without threatening to die. Technically, we could have driven to Stonehenge in around four hours in one go. It was more the car than anything that required we drag the journey into a multi-day road trip.

"Where are we going to sleep?" I asked, hoping to God the answer wasn't "the car."

"The car." Jeanne shrugged. At my expression, she added, "Or wherever. I haven't really thought about it."

"Of course you haven't," I sighed. "Well . . . I have relatives in Newmarket, which is, what, an hour away? We could crash with them."

Jeanne nodded, tearing her attention away from a group of boys walking past and finally focusing on the map. "And I've got mates in London. Sorted."

I dragged a highlighter down a motorway connecting us with Stonehenge, thinking how weird it was that Jeanne had friends outside of Norfolk. Barely anyone else I knew had a life involving anything not directly connected to our village.

*But now I will.*

I smiled a little, relishing the idea. Now that the initial surprise had worn off, studying our route, I felt a rush of excitement. How cool would it be to say I'd visited *Stonehenge*? And via a road trip—without parents—at that.

I relayed this to Jeanne, who gave me a tight hug. Her eyes sparkled as she said, "See? I didn't want to have to *actually* kidnap you, so I'm glad you're on board."

She went on to explain how she'd planned the trip (Jeanne made plans?) after reading about the solstice celebrations in some new-age magazine of hers. After running the idea by both of our parents, she'd packed and decided to pick me up on the way so that I'd be more likely to stay with her. Hence the crazy speed— the farther away from Castle Acre we were before I discovered her plan, the better.

"So how long would you have left it before telling me?" I asked, folding up the map and following her out of the rotunda.

"Until we were out of the county. Maybe longer."

I scowled.

We wasted about another hour in Swaffham, with me picking up all the supplies Jeanne had forgotten, and Jeanne browsing the local boutiques. The town wasn't known for being high-fashion, but Jeanne's new style involved the avant-garde rather than the trendy. As she rummaged through the racks at the back of a thrift shop, I began to wonder whether or not I should invest in more solstice-appropriate clothes. I was still a jeans-and-tee kind of girl.

Jeanne finished up with her purchases, we grabbed a couple of colas for the road, and climbed back into the car.

"I think it needs a name. The car, I mean," she said, running her hands over the vinyl seats thoughtfully. "Any car with character worth a penny has a name, right?"

"The Magic Lamp," I suggested. When Jeanne frowned at me like I was crazy, I explained, "Your nickname. Genie. Aladdin and the magical lamp the genie lives in."

"I don't like having a nickname," she scoffed.

"You call me *Tree*."

"Morris," she said as though she hadn't heard me. "Because it's a Morris Traveler."

"Wow." I rolled my eyes. "Your originality never ceases to amaze me."

"Shut up." She started the engine, cringing alongside me as an unhealthy wheezing sound accompanied the gesture. "I think it's cute."

"I think it's clichéd."

Jeanne winked, reversing out of the parking space without a backward glance. "You still haven't got the memo, eh Tree? I don't care what you think. Never have."

– – –

The car—I refused to refer to it as "Morris"—was remarkably comfortable as we drove southward into Suffolk, a county as full of farmland and quaint parishes as Norfolk. Well, except for a spell where my window got stuck right when the sun was beating down on my side of the car, causing my legs to practically melt into the vinyl. Plunging into the shade of Thetford Forest was a welcome change. Thick, green foliage blocked out the sky, houses and churchyards were replaced with abandoned campsites experiencing a brief period of vacancy before summer holidays. Half of me wanted to ask Jeanne to stop and simply camp out here for three days, playing "it" in the trees like we all used to as kids.

The forest bled out into more farmland. Yellow fields of oilseed, muddy fields filled with pigs, green fields filled with cows. Nitro Deluxe booming from the cassette player. A windmill, signs indicating a nearby historic property. Frankie Goes to Hollywood and George Michael blared on the cassette player.

We cruised down the motorway with relative ease,

still too early to experience the full summer rush. I folded up the map and closed my eyes, tapping my foot along to the beat of the music. Then, what felt like seconds later, I was wrenched back into reality by the sound of Jeanne swearing. Traffic had begun to queue approaching a small town, and when trying to slow, her gears had become stuck. When she had been able to slow down, she'd done it so violently that the car behind her screeched to a stop and started honking. Without consulting me, Jeanne found the next exit and turned in the opposite direction of the traffic.

"What's this road called?" I asked, craning my neck to try and catch a glimpse of any signs. "I'm losing us on the map."

That, and I was beginning to feel queasy. Navigation on-the-go had never been my strong suit. At least following main roads was simple.

"Um . . . we just passed Mildenhall."

I fought back the urge to snap, "*Obviously.*" Mildenhall was a massive air force base populated completely with Americans serving their overseas posting. Apparently they threw good parties that had a huge imbalance of guys to girls, but I'd never managed to snag an invite. It was absolutely colossal, impossible to miss.

"Badlingham!" Jeanne crowed, pointing at the sign as she turned down an ever-narrowing lane. "Badlingham Road. Got it?"

I squinted, fighting back the nausea. "We're on the wrong side of the motorway."

"Darn. We're heading in the right direction though."

"Yeah, but like three miles too far north." I reached around and shut off the music, silencing John Farnham midway through the chorus of his newest song. "Why don't you find somewhere to pull in? It's nearly sundown and we haven't eaten anything, so stopping and getting everything together is probably a good idea."

"Can't be. I didn't come up with it," Jeanne teased. Still, she eased off the accelerator, slowing right down and focusing more on where she was.

The road stretched out for ages in front of us, bordered on one side by meadows and a strip of trees on the other. The pavement was riddled with potholes and was barely wide enough to accommodate us, so that a car coming in the opposite direction would probably have to drive into the hedge to get by. Not a building was in sight.

"This is practically a path," Jeanne admitted. "Perhaps the motorway would've been better."

*You don't say.*

The trees materialized on the other side of us too, increasing the sense of tightness. As Jeanne slowed down to a crawling pace, I noticed I was holding my breath.

We crept over a tiny bridge, so constricted that both wing mirrors scraped the brick. Then, as though we weren't in enough of a pickle, the lane decided to fork into two unpaved . . . tracks. The word "road," even "lane," was too generous.

Jeanne stopped. "Well . . . crap."

"Crap, indeed," I nodded. "The route on the left looks like it's made of it."

According to the map, we'd come about a mile since turning, and there was at least another mile left in either direction before civilization returned. At this rate, noting the golden sunset, it would be dark before we were back where we were supposed to be.

"Sorry, Tree," Jeanne sighed, sounding genuine. "I think we're stuck."

"Don't worry," I said with as much brightness as I could muster. "Take the right-hand leg. Left looks like it's just for tractors."

"No." Jeanne shook her head, still sounding apologetic. "I mean, we're really, actually, completely, fully, and even utterly stuck." She revved the gas to prove it.

With a sinking feeling, I realized she hadn't stopped on purpose.

We both unbuckled and got out to survey the damage. One wheel was jammed in a pothole, and the other three were several inches deep in mud, which had splattered up the side of the car like it was part of the paintwork. Stuck.

Jeanne glanced at me. "Ideas?"

"Er . . . no."

We stared at the car dumbly, shuffling our feet and occasionally doing something useless, such as tapping the bonnet or kicking the tires. The sun continued to sink, shadows from the trees lengthening and drawing goose bumps on my arms. Considering we'd only been going an hour, this was a bit of an ominous start.

We tried pushing the car out, to no avail. Eventually, Jeanne had to turn the headlights on, given that there weren't any streetlights or buildings. I searched under the seats for the premade sandwiches and crisps we'd bought in Swaffham, sneaking one of Jeanne's scarves out of her suitcase in lieu of a proper jacket. Although there was nothing particularly sinister about the area, its pure remoteness had me on edge. We hadn't passed anyone else since turning off the main road, and I couldn't hear the hum of the motorway anymore.

"Someone will come by," I said, more to assure myself than anything. "Sooner or later."

"I guess we'll be sleeping in Morris after all." Jeanne wrapped her arms around her torso and shivered, walking a little way up the road and back again. "It's going to be a long night."

"Prawn mayonnaise or egg and cress?" I asked, holding up the sandwiches. "And I've got either cheese and onion or ready salted for crisps."

Jeanne considered this for a moment. "Prawn and ready salted. Ta very much."

The twilight was silent, broken only by the sound of us crunching and rustling the bags. When we were finished, small talk was exchanged to hide how nervous we were getting. An owl hooted from somewhere nearby, making both of us jump out of our skins, and Jeanne dived for the car.

"Come on, come on," she snapped, revving the engine again and again. It spluttered with effort, the wheels spinning frantically, but didn't move an inch.

She slammed the door and began storming down

the darkening lane ahead, muttering, "Screw it," under her breath.

"Jeanne?"

"There's got to be a house around somewhere." She kept walking. "We can phone for help. I am *not* staying out here all night."

I followed, pulling the scarf tighter around my shoulders and trying not to trip over potholes made invisible by the dimness. England wasn't known for its vicious animals—I was pretty sure cows were statistically the most dangerous things we had—but I couldn't help imagining that each rustle or screech belonged to something stalking us. Wolves, or bears, or a large stray dog perhaps . . .

"Hey!" Jeanne exclaimed, so suddenly I almost screamed. She glanced at me and chuckled. "Relax, Tree. Is that building what I think it is?"

I squinted, just able to make out the silhouette of a house or barn in the middle of a field, behind the row of trees. "There aren't any lights on."

"No, no, no." She grinned one of those grins that

always made me apprehensive. "Elm House, Suffolk. Isn't that supposed to be right around this area? This could totally be it!"

"Doesn't ring a bell."

"Supposedly one of the most haunted buildings in the east. The last family to live in it abandoned it, like, ten years ago after their son got possessed and tried to kill them. Some ancient demon lives in the attic walls. I think." Jeanne's grin widened. "Last year, I heard of this girl who went in on a dare and never came out. They found her body bricked into a secret room . . . or was it nailed to a doorway?"

"That is," I said, "without a doubt, the fakest thing I've ever heard. Ever."

Jeanne crossed into the field, gesturing at me to follow her. "In that case, we should be perfectly fine to go inside."

"That's trespassing! And besides, you were the one too scared to stay in the car a minute ago."

She waved her hand dismissively. "This is fun. Are you coming or not?"

I hesitated, looking over my shoulder at the dark lane behind and then at Jeanne, now running through the field toward the derelict house. *Crap.*

Taking a deep breath, I jogged to catch up.

# Chapter Three

CASTLE ACRE WAS KNOWN FOR TWO THINGS: ITS titular castle and its nine-hundred-year-old priory. The castle was ruined beyond recognition, but the priory still had enough walls left standing to give the illusion of being a proper building. There were stairs leading to nowhere, doors that had been locked for longer than anyone could remember, attics with no windows, and walls so thick they were practically soundproof. Of course, it was only natural that ghost stories involving headless monks and strange lights within inaccessible rooms sprang into being. It became a rite of passage to sneak in at night with friends and scare each other silly. When I was fourteen, before I'd known Jeanne, I'd gone to the priory at Halloween with my schoolmates, an episode that had ended with us all running home screaming after seeing a "body" hanging from the highest ruin. Apparently, a group of older kids had also snuck in, pantsed a younger boy, and thrown his trousers onto said tower. They'd remained there for weeks after.

Approaching Elm House, it wasn't hard to fathom how rumors of its being haunted spread either. Compared to the tiny flint cottages we'd passed on the journey here, it was massive, two full stories with windows peeking out of the collapsing roof. The outside was whitewashed stone rather than brick or flint, in dire need of repainting, and an entire side had been taken over by a jungle of ivy and brambles. The windows were boarded up, the front door was missing altogether, and the paved path leading up to it was so badly cracked that each piece gave the impression of being a miniature tombstone.

"'Elm House'," Jeanne read. "'Do Not Enter.' Sweet."

Standing at the threshold, I couldn't help but notice again how isolated we were. There was no telephone line or electricity in the house, and if anything were to happen . . .

"Jeanne!" I hissed, diving in. "Wait for me!"

She stood in the foyer, doing a full turn with her head tilted upward to take it all in. The staircase wrapped around the entrance and disappeared into the darkness above.

"It smells like mold," she said, wrinkling her nose. "Mold and my grandmother."

"With a slight touch of demons and death," I added. "It's freezing in here. Can we go now?"

"I think we should spend the night," Jeanne said in a tone that offered no room for debate. "Just to say we did. Attic or main floor?" Without waiting for me to answer, she started up the staircase, each movement unleashing an unhealthy creaking that seemed to come from the entire house at once.

Given three wishes, at that moment, my first demand would have been a light, without hesitation. The stairs felt just as rotten as the floor below, and on several occasions, something small scurried past my ankles and disappeared. I wasn't afraid of spooks, but the sheer amount of creepy crawlies that the house must have been hiding was more than enough to set my heart hammering. That, and it felt one wrong move away from collapsing entirely.

By the time I reached the next floor, my eyes had somewhat adjusted to the gloom. There was a threadbare carpet on the floor, covered with a suspicious blackish-red stain, but apart from that all the rooms appeared vacant. Out of a shattered bedroom window, I saw the moon had risen over the surrounding farmland.

"Can you see how to get up to the attic?" Jeanne whispered, hushed by weight of the stillness.

"Down the corridor, I'm guessing. Can't we stay down here?"

"Might as well go all the way. If it's too freaky, we

can come down again," she promised. "But I want to at least have a look."

We tiptoed down the corridor. I kept my eyes glued to the floor in front of me, fearful of what I'd find if I looked around too closely. Jeanne's presence was never far behind me, close enough that I felt her breathing down my neck several times.

"Here!" she exclaimed . . . from in front of me.

"Were you ahead the whole time?" I asked.

"Of course."

I shivered. It must have been a draft, although I heard footsteps coming from behind. *Stop it. You're letting it get to you.*

The passage leading up to the attic was straight out of a horror movie. Only wide enough to accommodate one person at a time, it climbed upward for at least thirty rickety steps into a swath of darkness so thick it made the entrance hall feel like daytime. The walls were scratched as though . . . as though something with extraordinarily long and sharp nails had dragged its hand all the way up.

I gulped.

"If we die," Jeanne said seriously, "then I want you to know you've been a suitably mediocre best friend. And I love you dearly."

"You've been okay, too. A solid six out of ten." I was alarmed by how dry my throat was. "If you die, can I keep this scarf? It's actually super warm."

"Fine, but I get your twelve-inch record collection," she laughed, forgetting she was supposed to hate my pop music now. "Ready?"

"You first."

The moment I said it, I regretted that order. Being behind was almost worse, feeling that odd presence breathing down my neck . . . at least Jeanne had me watching her back. The walls were claustrophobically close together, cold to the touch and remarkably solid compared to the rest of the house.

"Watch the next step, it's wonky."

"Watch the ghost, it's right in front of you," I retorted.

I felt, rather than saw, her eyes roll.

Reaching the attic, I let out the breath I'd been holding in. Moonlight streamed in from a gaping hole in the roof, a collection of decaying beams draped with so many spider webs it looked fake. There was a pile of litter, presumably from the last group of teenagers who'd decided to break in, but aside from that, the attic held nothing but dust.

Jeanne walked around, her flowing skirt and blond hair eerily ghostlike. She trailed her fingers over the walls, the beams, the graffiti, a smile tugging at her lips.

"You know, it's actually quite cool up here. If it was closer to home, I'd make it my permanent hangout."

I stretched my neck to see out of the hole. The view was amazing, with miles of black fields and the glowing mass of a village visible just before the horizon. Out here, in the middle of nowhere, the stars were bright and sparkling.

Jeanne lay down with a sigh, positioned so she too could see the stars. "Yeah, much better than Morris."

I swept the floor with my foot, then lay down too, using the scarf as a blanket. "Sweet nightmares."

"Don't let the demons bite."

My eyelids were heavy. It must have been close to midnight, and contrary to the stereotype surrounding people my age, I rarely stayed up much past ten. So despite being in a haunted house, sleep came quickly.

– – –

I woke up what simultaneously felt like hours and seconds later to Jeanne shaking my arm. Her face was pale and worried.

"What?" I twisted over and stared at the moon. Morning was still hours away.

"Can't you hear that?"

"Very funny," I grumbled, propping my head up on my elbow. "What is it, a voice telling us to—"

"Shh!"

We both froze. Faintly, almost inaudibly, there was the sound of piano music. Not very good music, just the sort of elementary-level plonking you'd expect from a beginner. "Twinkle, Twinkle, Little Star" type stuff, but that made it all the more unnerving.

"Did you see a piano on the way in?"

I shook my head, heart beginning to pound again.

The music was getting steadily louder, more violent. Gradually transitioning from lullaby to the sound that would result from repeatedly bashing someone's head against the keys.

Jeanne mouthed a curse.

Louder, louder, more chaotic, until it was a wonder the player hadn't broken the piano. Louder, louder.

My heart was practically humming. I gathered the scarf tighter around my shoulders and prayed I was actually still asleep.

Then it stopped. Just like that.

"Oh my god."

"What do we do?"

Jeanne thought for a moment, tapping her foot in a clear display of nerves. "Morris. Just keep your head down and run, and don't stop until we're back on the road. Sound like a plan?"

I nodded uncertainly. There had to be a reasonable explanation. Such as . . . such as . . .

"Tree!" Jeanne grabbed my arm and tugged me to my feet. If she'd been a dog, her ears would have been pricked up, alert. "It's probably an old tape left by locals or . . . well, it doesn't matter. Let's go."

I followed in her wake, body tensed in anticipation for the piano to strike up again.

*SLAM.*

Jeanne and I halted, exchanging looks of terror. The door, hanging by its hinges before the staircase, was now shut.

"Wind," Jeanne whispered. We both glanced outside, where the night was still and silent.

"Go on, then. Open it."

Jeanne was regarding the door like it might bite her. Gingerly, standing as far away as she could, she stretched out an arm and rattled the handle.

"Oh god." She rattled it again, more aggressively. "It's locked. It's *locked.*"

"Jammed, more like." I swallowed a growing panic and stepped forward. The handle was rusted and rough under my hand, in the same state of disintegration as the house itself. However, beyond a doubt, it was locked.

Jeanne swore, this time very much audibly.

"For the record, I blame you for this," I said. Joking aside, I felt scared enough to vomit.

Jeanne kicked the door with her combat boots, throwing all her weight behind it. I considered climbing out of the hole in the roof if she was unsuccessful.

Finally, on the fifth kick, it gave way. Unfortunately, no sooner had the door been crushed, the piano music sounded.

"It's not real." Jeanne's hand snaked through the darkness and gripped mine. It was unusually clammy.

"But let's call it a day," I agreed.

Down the stairs. Heart in my mouth. Jeanne

holding my hand in a vice grip. Stumbling blindly, tripping down the last few steps.

Scratching. Now that the piano had faded yet again, I could hear a horrible scratching noise coming from downstairs. My mind jumped to the marks on the wall.

"What is *that?*"

"The demonic entity. For once, I rather wish I hadn't been right."

"I'm serious, Genie."

Jeanne swallowed. "So am I."

A crash echoed from the foyer, followed by what sounded like the last remnants of a human scream after your throat has been screamed raw. One last, final shriek that was practically a death rattle.

Jeanne and I lost it. We both started screaming, too.

Hand on the wall, ignoring the sensation of brushing against mildewy wallpaper and spider webs, I rushed down the main staircase as fast as my shaking legs would allow. The blood roaring in my ears blocked out the other grisly noises, noises I realized we were running right toward . . .

The front door was right there. I could smell the fresh night air. Soon it would all be nothing but a bad memory.

Then I stubbed my toe on a nail protruding from a floorboard and tripped right over.

"Dang it, Tree!"

I grabbed her hand and hauled myself to my feet, and—

Wait. The hand was far too big to belong to Jeanne.

I yelped and jumped away from the shadowy figure, back pressed against a wall. I couldn't see Jeanne anywhere. Two silhouettes, coming closer and closer and closer and oh crap I was going to die and oh no oh no . . .

With one final burst of adrenaline, I balled my hand into a fist and swung out at the closest figure. Contact.

A male voice cried out in pain. Jeanne was calling my name.

Then a light flared up. Blinded, I stumbled backward and collapsed.

– – –

Dimly, I was aware of someone still screaming. Jeanne.

I sat up, rubbing my eyes. Every time I blinked, white lights flashed behind my eyelids.

The house looked a lot different now that I could see. The wallpaper still retained the barest trace of cabbage roses, and shabby lace curtains hung from every window; at some point, an elderly lady had obviously lived here. Flowery was a more accurate descriptor than haunted.

"Jeanne . . . ?" I mumbled, standing up.

She wasn't screaming in fear anymore. She was clearly angry. It didn't take long to find out why.

Two young men were also standing in the foyer, one of them gripping a substantial torch, its beam illuminating all the dust dancing through the air. It was hard to see much in the dimness, but they looked our age. One was taller, broader, and bleach-blond, aviator sunglasses perched atop his head. The thinner one had dark hair, almost black, and an unseasonably heavy leather jacket.

"See?" Ray-Ban said with a careless gesture in my direction. "She's fine. No harm done."

"Fine?" Jeanne snarled. "Fine? You nearly frightened us to death!"

"Mildenhall?" I asked. All heads swung to look at me. I think I was still dazed. "Your accent . . . you sound American. Are you from Mildenhall?"

"Yes, ma'am," Ray-Ban grinned. "Chris Shapland, from Cincinnati. Fighter pilot."

"Ritchie," said the other boy. "And ditto, except from Los Angeles."

Over their shoulders, I saw a grand piano in the far corner of an adjacent room.

"It was you," I said dumbly. "The piano and the locked door and the scratching . . . "

Chris exhaled a cloud of smoke. "Sorry. We came here with the same idea—assuming you were hoping for a ghost or two—and were sadly disappointed. We heard you ladies come in and didn't want you to have the same lame experience."

"So you decided to scare us." Jeanne's arms were folded, her eyes dark and flashing. Except I knew her too well—she wasn't furious at all. Well, maybe a little bit, but angry Jeanne was a very different person. She was trying to elicit another kind of apology here.

Ritchie shrugged. "In our defense, it was hilarious. Well worth the three hours of waiting."

Jeanne told him to do something that made even me blush. He simply blinked.

I was now aware of how I must've looked compared to her. The sun had faded her hair and teased out her freckles, and with her fierce expression and skirts the color of the rainbow, I felt awfully dull in comparison. I mean, I was the kind of pretty that got pointed out to you by an aunt at family gatherings. The sort that polished up nicely with a bit of makeup and mousse, both of which I was lacking at the present time. My shirt was rumpled and creased from sleeping in it, and I still had Jeanne's scarf wound round my neck. And of course, my hair, only now beginning to fade back to brown after a disastrous stint with mauve dye, completed the effect.

"You punched me," Chris said matter-of-factly.

"What did you expect?"

He chuckled. "Fair point. Look, girls, I'm sorry. It was only supposed to be a bit of fun. Can we make it up to you?"

I caught Jeanne stifling a smirk. *Jackpot.*

"Our car is stuck," I said before she could say anything. "In the morning, maybe you could have a go at fixing it?"

Chris glanced at Ritchie. "Sure. It's only fair."

Ritchie shrugged, then nodded. "All right."

Chris offered us his torch, insisting they had another one, and I dragged Jeanne back upstairs. Macabre shadows created by the light were still unnerving, and curling up in a vacant bedroom, I continued to flinch every time something made a sound. Jeanne didn't go to sleep for ages, muttering about the boys and how she'd suspected it was all a prank, et cetera, et cetera, long after I'd closed my eyes.

I woke up again at the crack of dawn to find the room bathed in a pinkish glow. Jeanne, thank goodness, hadn't yet strayed downstairs. She was blindly fixing her hair, frowning at nothing in particular.

"It's freezing," I yawned, shivering. "Seriously, feel my nose. It's like an ice block."

"D'you reckon they have food?"

"What?"

"The boys," she said, somewhat impatiently. "Food. I'm starving."

Even if they did, I wasn't sure if I wanted any. I didn't trust them in the slightest, even if they were good looking . . .

*Oh stop*, I chided myself. *You're pathetic.*

*But they're American fighter pilots—how much cooler can you get?*

Jeanne distracted me by lacing her boots on again

and strutting toward the stairs, face set in that same haughty, untouchable-yet-coy expression she'd been wearing last night. Game face.

"Morning," Chris greeted after we'd come downstairs. The Ray-Bans were covering his eyes now, a leather jacket and a knapsack flung over a broad shoulder. "Sleep well?"

"Shockingly, much better after you two decided to stop being such prats," Jeanne sniffed. "Although I could do with some breakfast right about now."

"They're fixing the car," I said uncomfortably. "We'll stop at a Tesco or newsagent's instead. Don't push it."

"Punishment," Jeanne whispered. "I'll milk it for as long as I can."

That was how we ended up eating miniature boxes of Coco Pops on our way to the car. The sunshine was warm and welcoming, completely transforming a landscape that had seemed so threatening in the darkness. Despite the early morning chill, it was shaping up to be a scorcher.

"So," Chris asked, "where are you two ladies from? You," he focused on Jeanne, "don't sound local."

"Wales, originally. We're both from Castle Acre."

"That's a long way to come to visit a condemned shack."

"It wasn't part of the plan," I grumbled.

Chris laughed, tossing his head so the sun glinted off his white hair. Like Jeanne, I was certain he knew exactly what he was doing down to every last twitch. Moving with a saunter, speaking with a drawl, challenging us to suggest anything he did wasn't pure gold.

The car was parked, completely illegally, in the middle of the lane. There were tire marks indicating somebody had squeezed around it overnight.

Ritchie raised an eyebrow, looking from the car in all its old purple-paint-and-wood-trimmed glory to Jeanne and back again. A ghost of a smile played across his lips before vanishing into a scowl again.

Chris whistled. "That's pretty, uh . . . vintage. Whose is it?" We stared, and he conceded, "Okay, stupid question. Little Miss Wales, I'm supposing."

"Jeanne," she corrected. "And yes, mine."

We stood in the shade of the trees, watching as the boys circled the car curiously.

"It's stuck," Ritchie said.

"God, you're a genius." Jeanne sighed. "Of course it's flipping stuck."

Ritchie's face reddened.

In the end, they determined that mechanics had nothing to do with the car's predicament. So all four of us gathered around the rear of the vehicle and leaned our weight against it, pushing and pushing until it rolled out of the pothole. Jeanne fired up the engine (which, it turned out, was nearly out of petrol) and triumphantly drove forward.

"There's a pump in Newmarket, if you can make it that far," Chris added.

"How did *you* get out here?" Jeanne asked, in lieu of thanks.

"Motorcycles."

I fiddled with the tape player, waiting for Jeanne to drive forward. I'd said goodbye already.

"You know," she said, more awkward than usual, "you're welcome to come with us. The more the merrier, after all."

*Oh please, no. Or yes.* I had a very strange feeling inside.

They looked at each other.

"Where are you headed?" asked Chris.

"Stonehenge. Summer solstice." She was testing the waters. Gauging if they would be turned off by that, as though the skirts and '60s Morris Traveler hadn't been enough of a hint. "We're stopping once more on the way, probably in London."

Pretending to stay occupied with the cassettes and the maps, I avoided checking their reactions. The silence seemed to stretch on forever.

"I can call a mate if we find a telephone," said Chris, slowly. "He'll take the bikes back in his trailer. What do you think, Ritch?"

"I suppose it's an English thing we haven't done yet," he replied without enthusiasm.

Should I have said something? Pointed out that

they didn't have spare clothes, or that riding in the rear seats was nothing short of torture? Elbow Jeanne and remind her that this was supposed to be a fun thing for just the two of us friends? They'd change the entire mood of the trip; Jeanne would keep acting to impress them, laughter would be replaced with embarrassment if anything went wrong, and I'd be stuck gaping at Chris's arms instead of the scenery.

"We're on break now," Chris said. "Just finished six weeks of intensive training. We were planning on road tripping around anyway, weren't we?"

Ritchie shrugged.

Of course, this entire charade was also all for show. They were going to come. With a girl like Jeanne at the helm, why wouldn't they jump at the chance to get on board?

Feeling as though I wasn't quite awake, I found myself getting out of the car so the boys could climb through to the back. Then, with a rather excessive revving of the engine, we were speeding down the lane toward the horizon.

# Chapter Four

$I$T DIDN'T TAKE LONG TO CLEAR THE LANES AND finally reunite with the motorway. The sky was a watercolor of pinks and faint blues, not a cloud in sight, and the road stretched in front of us without even the suggestion of a traffic jam. Our tank was full, we'd sorted out provisions, we were on a clear course to London . . . and yet, as I'd predicted, these things were pretty much just background noise.

Things weren't as awkward as I'd expected. They liked the same music as us, seeming somewhat relieved when Jeanne put on regular pop. They had the same sense of humor—well, Chris did. Ritchie simply looked less moody every now and then. Chris would crack jokes whenever the car acted up, and even called Jeanne out on her wacky driving when she kept switching between motorway lanes.

"You ever tried slalom skiing?" he asked. "Basically what you're doing, but on skis and going downhill."

"You see any hills around here?" she retorted, still swerving.

"I think he was kidding, Genie."

"Not entirely." Chris pulled a face. "It takes talent to do what she's doing and not vomit. You must be immune by now, Tree."

"Impossible."

He laughed. "I get it. So, anyway: Stonehenge. What gives with that?"

Jeanne smiled at no one in particular. "I saw pictures of last year's solstice in one of my magazines. It looked ever so magical. Like, there were quite literally real witches and stuff everywhere, and apparently you could feel the magic in the air . . . " She sighed. "It's going to be such an amazing experience, you wait and see."

"Is it going to be crowded?" Chris asked.

"Doubt it. Not many people are into this sort of stuff anymore."

"I wonder why," Ritchie muttered, speaking for the first time.

"You know, Ritchie here holds the record for the fastest biker at Mildenhall." Chris leaned forward, resting his arms on both of our seats. We were driving down an exceptionally unexceptional piece of road with nothing whatsoever to look at, so I found myself clinging onto his every word. His accent was almost hypnotic. "Round about a hundred miles an hour, wasn't it?"

"Easy," Ritchie scoffed through a wad of gum. I'd noticed he only chewed on the left side of his mouth.

"How do you know he was the fastest?"

"There's a stretch of road by the base," Chris explained, pleased by my interest, "that ends in a sharp bend. So all the guys with bikes—and that's a good few—set a timer to see how long it takes the other riders to get from the beginning of the road to clearing the corner. Most slow down 'cause they're scared of skidding, but not Ritchie. Nearly scraped his ear, the bike was so close to the ground."

Jeanne whistled. "That's a really stupid way to get killed."

"True," Chris laughed, "but not nearly as stupid as the timer. Someone has to play passenger so they can hold the stopwatch."

"And that's you?"

"Of course."

It was easy to picture. Ritchie in his black leather jacket, screaming down a lane on a bad-boy motorcycle, and Chris wearing his Ray-Bans, laughing as he held on with only one hand at a hundred-plus miles an hour.

"You girls will have to come with us one day." He glanced at Ritchie for confirmation. "See what real speed feels like."

I shuddered. "I'll pass, thanks. I can barely stomach roller coasters."

Chris nodded, as though I'd confessed something odd but admirable, and said, "I've always been a speed junkie. That's why I became a pilot. Well, that wasn't always the plan, until . . ."

The stories kept on coming. Tales of encounters with Russian fighters, near-death experiences, harrowing mechanical failures, and performing for the Queen on her birthday. How he'd met Ritchie after they'd both been stranded at Heathrow Airport, alone in a new country, and been best friends ever since. They'd been to the Live Aid concert; they'd spoken with several leading pop stars; they'd been extras in an episode of a popular soap opera; they'd ridden bicycles to Land's End, the most westerly point of England, and back . . . the list went on and on. By the time Jeanne announced we were stopping for snacks, I felt like I'd lived another, more exciting life through them. Mine was so boring in comparison I was almost embarrassed.

"It's eleven o'clock, leaches," Jeanne announced. She'd adopted the endearing name after none of us coughed up for petrol. "Do we just want snacks, or lunch?"

Approaching London meant that towns were becoming a much more common sight, so we decided to grab a meal while we were stopped and pick up essentials—i.e. crisps and cola—later on.

We were now in Essex, a county bordering north-eastern London, although the village could have easily fit into the Norfolk countryside. Typical flint cottages, winding streets, quaint little schoolhouses and churches, and, naturally, a selection of pubs. Jeanne liked the look of one called the Crown and Thistle, a ramshackle sixteenth century free house offering cheap meals and beer.

"Go ahead," Ritchie said as we made to go in. "I'll catch up with you."

Chris raised a white eyebrow. "Need to get some shopping done?"

Ritchie rolled his eyes.

The pub was nothing unusual. Oddly low ceilings, beams thicker than my legs, and a carpet that was a faded green and red, so rucked up in places that it was a wonder anybody could walk through without tripping. There were only a few tables clustered around the main bar, a massive wooden centerpiece made in a very medieval style with a barman who looked old enough to have carved the cupboards himself.

"It's so charming," Chris said after we'd taken our seats. "There's nothing like this in America."

"Charming?" Jeanne wrinkled her nose. "Your restaurants are so much cooler, though."

"Cheap burgers and soggy fries," Chris dismissed. "Nowhere near as good as—" he glanced at the menu "—battered cod and chips. Or sausage and mash. What are you having?"

I started, realizing he was directing the question at me rather than Jeanne. "Um . . . fish and chips, I think. Always a safe bet."

Ritchie returned and we all ordered the traditional fish and chips, with the exception of Jeanne, who asked for a very untraditional platter of calamari. The food took ages to arrive, so to pass the time, Chris told more stories about his adventures and misadventures as a pilot. Jeanne piled in with stories of her own that I'd never even heard before.

"Smile," said Ritchie when a less-than-apologetic waiter brought over our now-cold food nearly an hour later. "No, not you. These three."

"Only if you demonstrate," Jeanne winked, spurring a laugh from me and Chris.

Ritchie, naturally, remained deadpan. It turned out he'd purchased a cheap camera and several rolls of film from a local shop earlier, a gesture I found somewhat surprising. Ritchie fondly recollecting memories via a photo album was a weird concept.

"You with the purple hair," he snapped. "Smile."

"Oh." I blushed and smiled. There was a blinding flash, Ritchie nodded his approval, and we took that as a go-ahead to eat our lukewarm meals.

*Purple hair.* Compared to the sheen it had been, it almost looked brown again to me. I was too scared of messing up again to re-dye, but moments like this made me wish I had anyway.

The fish tasted like deep-fried cardboard, though the chips were greasy enough to redeem them. Chris declared they were still better than anything he'd eaten in America, using that as a platform to launch into a tale of how he'd been forced to catch and eat frogs after getting lost in the fens during a training exercise.

"You think that's gross?" Jeanne countered, wiping her mouth on the back of her hand—clearly we'd toned down the flirting by now. "Laverbread. Traditional Welsh breakfast dish. Seaweed and oatmeal. It literally looks like someone ate their own crap and vomited it up again."

"You have a way with words," remarked Ritchie, airily. "Remind me to try it before we leave."

– – –

Leaving the village, Jeanne stalled a grand total of three times. Instead of getting flustered, she laughed it off with the guys. We cruised through more farm-land, prying all the windows open and bearing the pungent, agricultural air in return for relief from the heat. Chris begged us to stop outside a parish called Widdington so he could take a picture with us by the sign, citing that it sounded comically like "widdle," an English slang term he wanted to remember when he returned to the USA. Jeanne and I both scorned at how immature that sounded, but spent a good ten minutes posing with him anyway.

We'd barely been back in the car ten minutes when Chris swiveled around and asked us to stop. Assuming he'd seen another village sign that could be interpreted lewdly, I was surprised to see the sign in question was the brown, oak leaf-sporting one of the National Trust, the organization that owned a good chunk of historical properties and landscapes throughout the UK. It wasn't something you'd expect an army boy to take much interest in.

"What?" Jeanne asked, stopping in the middle of

the road and reversing to catch a glimpse of the sign herself.

"I have a membership there," Chris said.

"And just like that, I'm ashamed to be your friend," Ritchie sighed. "Hopefully your uncoolness isn't contagious."

To my surprise, instead of laughing the jab off, Chris's face went red. I glanced at Jeanne, deciding I knew exactly how he felt.

"Do you really?" I asked.

"Yeah." He brightened and produced a slip of plastic bearing the same logo from the pocket of his jeans. "I won it in a game of poker. We were both stone broke, and this guy, Paul Albury, bet his National Trust membership. I think I bet three cans of tuna and four cans of baked beans."

"Okay, great," Ritchie said. "So what?"

"So we should check this place out. We've got time."

"First of all, none of the rest of us are members, and second of all, we literally stopped ten seconds ago," Jeanne pointed out. She still sat in the middle of the road, causing incoming traffic to honk madly and swerve to avoid hitting her. She didn't seem to notice.

"We'll be there too early at this rate. C'mon, they'll probably have ice cream. My treat," he wheedled.

"Oh," I tapped Jeanne's shoulder. "There's a police car coming up behind you."

Just like that, she decided that perhaps a stop at the National Trust wouldn't be such a bad idea after all. Doing a U-turn, she beamed at the officer on her way past and pulled into the gravel carpark of the property.

The property in question was Hatfield Forest, apparently an ancient hunting ground in use since medieval times. The trees here were massive and twisted and knotted, their spindly branches seeming far too thin in comparison; even I, who'd grown up next to the sprawling forest at Thetford, was wowed. Chris graciously opted to pay for us, given that it was his idea, on the condition that we didn't go crazy when ordering ice cream.

As with any English icon worth its weight, a Mr.

Whippy truck was parked only a few paces inside the gates. Despite having recently eaten, we all ordered ninety-nines—vanilla ice creams with a chocolate flake stuck in the top.

"Is this real ice cream?" Ritchie asked, glaring at his with an expression somewhere between distrust and barely concealed delight. "It tastes . . . odd."

We were all too busy eating ours to comment.

To pass time, glad to be off of the road again, we wandered through the expansive trail network. There were a few families with children too young to be in school gathered about, and a few elderly couples, but aside from that, we had the run of the place. I imagined it would be a beautiful place in autumn when all the leaves changed, and an eerie place in winter when there weren't any leaves at all. As it was, on the brink of summer, the canopy glowed golden as sun filtered through, casting speckles of light over the trail. It was the type of wood where goblins and fairies should live, the remnants of what had once spanned the entirety of Britain for longer than anyone could remember.

"We used to play 'It' all the time in a forest like this—well, not quite like this—and we'd always get lost," Jeanne said, licking the bottom of her cone where the ice cream was dripping. "Remember when we went out to Thetford in school, Tree? We played 'Fox and Hound,' and I was supposed to be a fox, but I pretended to be a hound so I could hide with you?"

"Only because you forgot your shoes and wanted to avoid running."

Out of nowhere, the trees melted away to reveal a small lake. It was stiller than a mill pond, perfectly reflecting the woodland around it. We found a bench, sat down, and finished off our ice creams.

"Ritchie and I grew up in cities," Chris sighed, "so we didn't really have school trips to places like this. It's a shame—I loved the outdoors when I was little."

"You don't anymore?"

"Well, yeah, but in a different way. 'Tag' doesn't quite hold the same appeal anymore." He sighed again, like he was genuinely saddened by this. "I can never be bothered."

"How inspiring," said Ritchie, dryly.

Jeanne stood up, spinning on the spot so her skirt swished around her ankles. "Tree and I still do crazy things, don't we, Tree? Spontaneity is our thing."

*Like this spontaneous kidnapping?* I cringed just thinking about all the "crazy" situations Jeanne had dragged me into, the recent experience in Elm House fresh in mind.

"Greenham Common?" Jeanne pushed, eyes sparkling with mischief. "This very January?"

"That name rings a bell," said Chris.

"RAF missile base, isn't it?" Ritchie frowned. "There's a women's protest camp that's been set up there for ages—I've seen it on the news."

Chris laughed. "Yeah, right. Of course you would know about an all-women's camp, even if they were campaigning for abstinence."

Ritchie glared at him. "Just because *you* never bother to read the papers."

Jeanne coughed, redirecting attention back to her. She had a story to tell. "*Anyway*, Tree and I were there in January. Only for, like, a day, but we helped take apart the perimeter fence during the night, which was especially funny 'cause the government thought the camp had been dismantled."

Again, I cringed. American cruise missiles had been kept at RAF Greenham Common since '81, and the protest had been ongoing for nearly as long. The idea of warheads so close to home was not something I embraced, in fact quite the opposite, but the consequences of being caught were terrifying—jail would've been the least of our worries. I think even Jeanne had second thoughts in the moment, but ever since, she'd regained enough confidence to brag every chance she got.

"Wow, if someone tried dismantling the perimeter at Mildenhall, they'd be shot on sight," Chris said with a nervous chuckle.

Jeanne grinned, twirling again like a child given a gold star. "It was a rush."

"Might I suggest a roller coaster?" Ritchie sighed, rolling his eyes and rising from the bench too.

"Not a high enough chance of death for Jeanne," I said.

"You were there too, were you not?"

"I'm always there," I muttered, "but rarely willingly."

"It was for a good cause," Jeanne shrugged.

"So make a poster. Circulate a petition. Don't dismantle a bloody Army perimeter." Chris wiped the remnants of ice cream and chocolate onto his jeans, regarding Jeanne with an expression that reminded me that he, ultimately, was part of what we'd been fighting against.

Jeanne must have sensed that the mood was veering away from what she'd wanted, so she gestured for us to follow her through the reeds to the lakeshore. There was barely enough room for the four of us to stand there, sandwiched between the reeds, bank, and water while ducks squawked at our feet. Chris tried skipping a pebble and failed miserably. I copied him and managed to skip three times.

"Overachiever," he said in mock disgust, nudging

my shoulder. My breath caught in my throat, which he wrongly interpreted. "Sorry, didn't mean to push you in."

"Oh, that's okay, I—"

"But I did!" Jeanne squealed, giving me a hefty shove so that I stumbled forward and plunged into the water.

For a second, I didn't even register what happened. Then, feeling the frigid water seeping into my clothes, my hands several inches deep in what could only be described as goop, I mouthed a curse and started yelling at Jeanne. Well, at least I would have, had she not purposely fallen backward into the water with me.

"*What?*"

"Weren't you all just complaining that you felt too grown up?" Jeanne floated on her back, her hair forming a halo around her head and shoulders. "Besides, it's far too hot in the sun."

"Chris was complaining, not me!" I cried, running onto the bank and shivering violently, wringing the water from my own hair. "This isn't a swimming pool!"

Chris, who had been watching our little exchange with barely concealed amusement, blinked at the sound of his name and gave Ritchie a stiff shove, trying to push him into the lake too. Ritchie, clearly anticipating this, stumbled but didn't fall over, grabbing Chris's outstretched arm and attempting to throw *him* in. A scuffle ensued, comical enough I forgot my anger for a moment.

There was an almighty splash as they both lost their footing at the same time and tumbled into the lake beside Jeanne.

"Join us," Jeanne said in a dead serious tone, reaching out a muddy hand toward me. "Complete your initiation."

I bent down and flicked water at her. "Thanks, but I've already been baptized into your church of stupidity. Driving to London is going to be freaking uncomfortable now!"

"I have clean clothes."

"No towel."

"I shall hang myself to dry in the sun, then." Jeanne stood up, her hair in rattails and her skirt heavy with dirty water. She flicked a glance at Chris and Ritchie, who also stood up and glowered good-naturedly at each other, and laughed. "Sorry, guys. I couldn't resist."

My jeans were tight enough that on occasion I'd had to undo the stitching and literally sew myself into them, so having them sopping wet was unbearably uncomfortable. We wound our way back through the woodland, brightly aware of the curious looks we were getting, and used the public bathroom to change into spare clothing. The boys didn't have that luxury, so they were forced to stand in the sun until they were as dry as possible. It really was something of a miracle that by the time we returned to the car, we were laughing about the episode rather than giving Jeanne the cold shoulder. Perhaps it was because despite all my previous doubts, the idea of looking like a drowned rat in front of the others wasn't something awful anymore.

— — —

Signs for London popped up all over the place, the distances ticking down bit by bit. Fields gave way to industrial estates, and antiquated villages were swallowed by full-sized towns. Eventually they would all bleed together to form one mass, a collection of council estates and factories and warehouses and condominiums that hid London proper in its heart.

And if the amount of larking about was anything to go by, despite my fears, we'd arrive bonded like we'd all been friends for ever and ever.

# Chapter Five

IT WAS MID-AFTERNOON WHEN WE PASSED HARLOW, one of the last major towns unconnected to London on this side of the city. We were singing along to U2's "With or Without You" at the top of our lungs— minus Ritchie, of course, who looked like he'd rather be anywhere else—causing other drivers to stare whenever we were stopped at traffic lights. The windows had jammed again, this time fully down, and so no one was spared from hearing our warbling.

"Whoops." Jeanne had been tapping the steering wheel in time to the beat and missed, accidentally slamming the horn and startling a nearby cyclist. "But seriously guys, we should start a band."

"Who the hell would be on vocals?" Ritchie drawled, sounding even more disdainful than usual. "I think that performance knocked years off my life."

Jeanne thought about this. "We're hot enough nobody'd care. I'll front, Tree can be my backup girl on the bass, and Chris can go crazy on the drums. We'll call ourselves . . . "

"Genie Goes to Stonehenge?" I suggested.

"J, T, and C." She sighed, ignoring me. "No vowels. No cool acronym possible."

"You're excluding Ritchie," Chris pointed out. He sounded hoarse from singing so loudly. "And, as a side note, No Cool Acronym Possible might work."

Ritchie turned to the window, chewing his gum aggressively.

"The funny thing is, he can actually sing," Chris mused. Ritchie shot him a death glare, but he continued, "No, really. Karaoke night down at Mildenhall. He just grabbed the microphone and belted his way through half the charts on a dare once. And the reason nobody stopped him was because he is amazing."

I twisted in my seat to face the boys, the crueler part of me enjoying having someone feel more awkward than me. Unfortunately, he did seem more irritated than awkward, but there were easy ways of fixing that. Jeanne hopped right to it.

"Sing for us!"

Ritchie tensed. "Um, no."

"Please!" I begged, squashing a smirk.

"Go on," Chris added. "For the ladies."

"What song? This one? Or this one?" Jeanne reached over and skipped through the tracks on her cassette player.

Ritchie's face continued to sour. "No."

We needled at him for a good while, until we realized it was a futile cause and left him alone. However, after we'd drained our colas and begun bellowing out more songs, if I listened carefully, I could have sworn I heard him quietly singing along, too.

Inevitably, after consuming so much cola, my

bladder soon felt fit to burst. By now there was almost no open countryside visible, only shopping malls and commercial buildings filling up spaces between houses, as though we'd started in the past and were steadily travelling farther and farther into the future as we approached London. In my opinion, everything was also growing uglier. Grayer, colder.

"Jeanne." I poked her. "Code yellow."

"Can you hold it? We're like twenty minutes out."

"Actually," Ritchie said, in the same deadpan tone, "I second that code."

"Well, in that case."

In this part of the country, it was more a question of choosing facilities than finding them. We were staying with distant cousins of Jeanne's in Watford, on the western side of London, so we'd taken a route that guided us northward rather than directly through the chaos of downtown. That meant there were plenty of suburban conveniences dotted all over the place. Pulling off the motorway, it wasn't long before we found a block of public toilets crammed between a treed park and an alley of derelict shops.

"Classy," Chris whistled. "Tell you what, why don't I stay with the car. I'm sure the locals are lovely people and all, but given the windows are open . . . "

"You're an angel. I think I'm going to stretch my legs in the park for a bit."

Jeanne had been complaining about her legs cramping up these last few miles, but I knew it was useless offering to take over. She'd never let anyone else drive.

The toilets were absolutely foul, covered in peeling paint, graffiti, and all manner of questionable substances. I was in and out as quickly as possible, not even bothering to check my makeup in the mirror. I even beat Ritchie. Chris was loitering outside the car, Ray-Bans perched on his nose, winking at a group of girls tottering past.

"I think they were giggling at the car, not you," I pointed out.

He jumped. "Probably."

I reached in through the passenger window

and grabbed the map—we were exactly halfway to Stonehenge. Even though we'd only left Castle Acre yesterday, it felt like we'd been on the road for ages. In a good way, of course.

Time passed. Chris was giggled at by another group of girls. I maintained my focus on the map for much longer than was necessary. Without Jeanne, the awkwardness between us increased tenfold.

"Ritchie must have fallen in," I observed.

"Yeah. Maybe I should go save him." He didn't move. Then, "Why does Jeanne call you Tree?"

"It's short for Teresa," I shrugged.

"Which do you prefer?"

Huh. I'd never been asked that before. I answered that I didn't mind either way, but given the choice, I liked my full name.

Chris nodded. "All right. Teresa, then." With that, he sauntered into the men's toilets.

He pronounced it teh-REEZ-uh as opposed to TREE-suh, like everyone else. Catching my reflection in the window, I realized I was wearing a stupid little smile.

Chris came back within seconds and announced Ritchie was nowhere to be seen. He didn't seem very concerned, and so neither was I. I volunteered to do a sweep of the surrounding area—for Jeanne as much as Ritchie—while he stayed with the car. I tucked the map away and moved toward the park.

It wasn't a particularly nice park. The trees were scraggly and partially dead, sporting just as many brown leaves as green ones, and a metal playground was being used by more squirrels than children. An overgrown trail wound its way past the crumbling brick exterior of the toilet block to a field, where two preteens were kicking a ball and ducking behind a bush whenever an adult walked past. Having graduated, it was funny thinking that most kids were still in school.

"Jeanne?" I called, causing the football players to freeze. "Where are you? I need you to help me find Ritchie."

Nothing. The park was a few acres at most, so I was surprised I couldn't see her. I yelled again. Scanned for a colorful flowing skirt, long blond hair, or abandoned boots. Nothing. It was like she'd vanished. Though perhaps we'd missed each other; she'd probably headed back to the car just as I'd set out to find her.

I made my way to the car again, enjoying the fresh air and shade. Then I saw her over by the wall, half obscured by an electrical box.

"Jeanne, you—"

I broke off. She wasn't alone.

Ritchie was there. With Jeanne, kissing her like there was no tomorrow. And she was kissing him back with enough fervor to make me automatically look away. Peering at them again, cheeks burning, I opened my mouth to say something, anything, but no sound came out save for a squeak. Both their eyes were closed, like those mushy movie couples. Should I do something? Say something?

*No. Are you mental?* There wasn't anything wrong with it. I was simply shocked. Not even really jealous.

It was probably the camera and the singing that cinched the deal for Jeanne.

"We should get going," I heard Jeanne say breathlessly, pulling away. "Before Tree sends out a search party."

*Bit late for that.*

"Fine." Ritchie didn't move. Jeanne didn't protest. Unable to bear it anymore, I turned and half-ran-half-walked from the park to the car.

"Did you find them?" Chris asked. His expression grew concerned. "Are you okay?"

"Yeah, um . . . " I managed to crack a grin, waving a hand to sum up all the words I was struggling to find. "Jeanne and Ritchie, er . . . they were kinda . . . "

"Kissing?"

I nodded.

Chris bobbed his head, as though he wasn't the least bit surprised. He'd expected it, even. "Ritchie acts like he's made of stone, but on the inside, he's just as human as the rest of us. I guess that makes it inevitable, then."

"Makes what?"

"Us," Chris said in the same unaffected tone. "If those two have hooked up, then the obvious next step is for the remaining singles—us—to do the same."

For a moment, all I could think of was Chris kissing me the way Ritchie had kissed Jeanne, passionate and fierce, uncaring of who saw . . . then I jerked back to reality. Because I was me, and that made it impossible.

"Um," I said stupidly.

"Logic," Chris shrugged. Had he always been standing so close? I could even smell him, a mixture of cologne and fish and chips.

"I've only known you a day!" I blurted, confused by the raging torrent of emotions in my head, my heart, everywhere. I felt dizzy. "It's ridiculous, just because Genie and Ritchie . . . I mean, in a few days we'll go our own ways and I can't . . . I've never even . . . and you . . ."

Chris's face fell. "Teresa, I wasn't being serious. It was just a joke. Like how in movies and everything . . . y'know." His cheeks were just as red as mine. "Sorry. I feel like an idiot now."

Oh.

My heart thudded once more in my ears, then fell silent. The alley was unnaturally still.

Of course he'd been joking. And embarrassment didn't even begin to cover how that made me feel.

"I'm sorry."

He looked miserable. "Me too. I didn't realize you—"

"No, no, I just—"

Jeanne and Ritchie chose that moment to reappear from the park. Ritchie was sporting his usual poker face, but Jeanne carried a silly smile. She either didn't pick up on my distress, or didn't care, walking straight past both of us and sliding into the driver's seat.

"You coming, Tree?"

No "Are you okay?" or any attempt to convey what had happened with Ritchie. Nothing of what you'd expect from a best friend.

I got in wordlessly and Chris did the same. The tension was almost palpable.

"Everybody buckled in?" asked Jeanne, absently. "Let's go, London calling."

# Chapter Six

IPRETENDED TO HAVE A HEADACHE, TURNING toward the window and not uttering a word. Chris was similarly silent, a dramatic change from earlier, but Jeanne filled the resulting void with a mixture of chatter and singing. As traffic built up, slowing us to a crawling pace, she gradually grew less sunny and more irritable.

"Stupid lorries," she growled. "Oi! Get out of the fast lane! You're a bloody hundred-ton lorry, not a bloody sports car!"

I squeezed my eyes shut. Every time she swerved, my head banged against the glass.

It was a miracle that in the forty-five minutes it took to arrive outside of Jeanne's friend's flat I managed not to throw up. When we arrived, I helped to haul our suitcases up several flights of stairs as if in a stupor, not registering our hosts' faces or names. Even the flat itself slid from my memory the second I stepped outside for some fresh air.

"Tree!"

I kept staring at a lamppost, waiting for it to turn on. It was the only one that hadn't yet.

"There you are." Jeanne tapped my shoulder. It hurt more than it should have. "Ashley says there's a great club down the road with a really good DJ. It's been a long day; I'm dying to unwind."

The idea of going to a crowded room full of sweaty people and booming music was appalling at the moment. Especially if Chris was going, too.

"Nah. Can we not?"

Jeanne stopped bouncing. Not because she was concerned about me, but because I was rejecting her idea. "Don't be a killjoy."

"I'm not. I just don't want to go. And anyway, if you're driving tomorrow, you probably shouldn't either."

"The law." She rolled her eyes and resumed bouncing on her heels. "You'll have to come and keep an eye on me, Tree, just in case."

"I'm not your *freaking* babysitter, Jeanne."

I regretted the words as soon as I'd said them. I hadn't meant to sound so bitter, hadn't meant to . . . yet at the same time, I'd wanted to say something to that effect for a very long time.

Jeanne went rigid. "Excuse me?"

I struggled between apologizing and pushing my point further. Everything was building up, everything I'd let fly over my head returning with vengeance. *"You still haven't got the memo, eh, Tree? I don't care what you think. Never have,"* she'd said. Not entirely a joke. She hadn't asked me if I wanted to come on this trip, because she needed a sidekick and didn't want to give me the chance to say no. Not because she genuinely wanted to give me a surprise. I hadn't wanted to go inside Elm House, yet we had anyway. She never asked me if it was okay for the boys to join us. Hell, unlike Chris, she'd never asked if I minded being called "Tree," no matter how strongly I hinted at disliking it. And here we were, alone, and she wasn't going to bring up the fact she'd been making out with Ritchie. I wasn't someone who she thought to confide in, and that hurt more than anything.

"I've had enough," I said, willing myself to look her in the eye, "of being bossed around by you. So go to your stupid club, but I think I'm going to go home."

Jeanne flinched as though I'd slapped her. Then her eyes narrowed. "Pardon me for making choices you're incapable of."

"You never give me a chance! It's always your way or the highway, and I'm sick and tired of it!" I cried. "Just because I think inside my head rather than aloud, it doesn't mean I need the likes of you to decide things for me. I'm fed up of being dragged around by you!"

"Thing is, if I didn't drag you around, you'd never have a life," she scoffed, folding her arms and leaning against the lamppost, which flickered twice before turning on and casting a spotlight over the path. "Look at you, dropping out the second things get out of your comfort zone. It's just a club, for Pete's sake!"

"That's exactly the point," I said, softer than before. "This isn't about the club, but you don't care enough to dig that deep. It always has to be about you."

She stared at me. One hand began twisting her hair, a nervous habit of hers, and I wondered if she ever noticed such quirks about me.

"You . . . " she trailed off and shook her head.

Voices echoed from inside the flat, and for a moment, we both turned our attention to the window, watching, saying nothing. I took a deep, steadying breath. I didn't want to do this; despite it all, Jeanne was still my best friend. We could talk it out like grown-ups.

Then she laughed and pivoted back inside. "Come on, Tree. I'm going to get ready."

My gut clenched. It was easy to imagine what she'd tell the boys: *It's just Tree being silly. Don't worry, she'll get over it. She gets all hissy when she's tired, nothing unusual . . . who's ready to party?*

There was only one thing for it. If I ever wanted to be taken seriously, I had to make good on my threat.

*Move, Teresa, move!* I shrieked at myself, willing my legs to walk in the other direction. To just once find the strength to stand up for myself with enough vigor that Jeanne actually noticed. But all the fire and bravery I'd managed to muster before was slinking away at a remarkable rate, and the pacifist part of me was wondering why I was trying to make trouble when there didn't have to be any.

"Tree, are you coming or not?" Jeanne yelled from the door. "Don't sulk, come on."

I hesitated, then, bitterly hating myself for it, followed her inside.

– – –

Perhaps she hadn't thought to pack food or maps, but I found my suitcase contained a perfect clubbing outfit: black tights, a miniskirt, and a fitted black blouse I hadn't had the courage to wear yet. I put it all on, deciding that if I was going to do this, I should at least do it properly. It all felt horribly tight: my clothes clinging like a second skin, the dollop of mousse Ashley (Jeanne's cousin, who was putting us up for the night) coated my hair in, the triumphant smirks Jeanne kept flicking in my direction. I don't think I'd ever been less enthusiastic about dancing.

"Oh, cheer up," Jeanne said, coming to share the mirror beside me. She was wearing a shimmering, silver mini-dress with floaty, off-shoulder sleeves, and looked sickeningly good. Her blond hair had been sprayed to give off an almost grungy image—artfully distressed. "You're tired, I get it. This will help. Trust me. Just smile." She demonstrated.

I didn't smile.

Chris and Ritchie, having no extra clothes, had cleaned up rather than changed. They both still looked *very* good, enough so that I momentarily forgot why I was in a foul mood. Then Jeanne waltzed in, smiling at Ritchie, and I soured.

We all piled into the car, the scent of hair product overwhelming, and followed Ashley's directions. The club was in another semi-urban area, right on the border of London proper, and located on the floor above a nail salon. The lineup of people outside was probably a good sign, I supposed. If I was trying to be positive.

The second we got out of the car, Jeanne and I were swarmed by groups of boys. It wasn't anything personal; the club wasn't letting groups consisting only of young men in, so their only way through was to pretend to be friends with the likes of us. Jeanne pretended to think about it, then agreed on the condition they bought her drinks. Nobody consulted me.

"You're eighteen, right?" Chris asked me when we were three groups back from the bouncer. It was the first time he'd spoken all night.

"Yup," I said. "I'm legal. Don't worry, I won't drag the group down."

*Wow, that sounded bitter.* I forced a grin, and he grinned uneasily back.

The club was typical of others I'd been to. Dim lighting, red velour sofas scattered around round tables, a bar, and a tiny dance floor crammed with bodies next to the DJ's table. Music thrummed through the speakers at such volume I felt my bones shaking. Most people there were around our age, dancing, chatting, and otherwise mulling about in the sea of shiny clothing and white, grinning teeth.

"Do me a favor," Jeanne said, leaning right into me so I could hear over the music, "wink if I look funny. Like, if my lipstick smudges or—"

"I know the drill."

"Good, good." She glanced over her shoulder, where the group of guys we'd brought in with us were hovering. "I'm gonna go cash in on some drinks. What do you want, Tree?"

I shook my head. "You're driving home, Genie."

She waved a hand. "Relax. Anyway, it isn't every night where the opportunity presents itself to have the most expensive drink on the menu courtesy of someone else."

I wanted to argue, but she'd already turned her back on me.

Great. Awesome.

Usually, I loved this sort of thing. The neon lights, the energy, the new remixes, the excitement of checking out local talent . . . but tonight, I just wanted to go home. I just wanted to go to sleep and wake up somewhere else.

"Buy you a drink?" some anonymous young man from Jeanne's pack asked, noticing I wasn't moving. "Or a dance?"

"But do you think I should still be here?" I asked, turning to him anxiously. "Am I being silly?"

"Um . . ."

"I mean, if you were me, what would you do? Would you suck it up or . . . ?" I shook my head. "Sorry. I'll dance."

Crammed in the pulsing mass of the dance floor, I tried unsuccessfully to lose myself in the music. I kept waiting for Jeanne, who knew I wasn't feeling right, to come and check up on me.

After a while, a slow song came on and I headed for the toilets. And, of course, Jeanne was there too.

"Oh, hey," I said automatically. "You too?"

"I'm not slow-dancing with some *creep*." The harsh lighting was unflattering, even on her. "That's what always happens."

"Look—" *Just talk it out.* "—I want to go now. I need to talk to you somewhere else, you—"

"There's a tear in your tights," she pointed out, overriding me. "The night is young, Tree, loosen up a bit. I'm sure whatever it is will be just as important tomorrow."

"You know full well what it is!" I hissed. "And no, I don't want to wait until tomorrow."

"You want to borrow my tights?" She snorted. "Oh, don't look at me like that. But seriously, you might want to change."

My hand shot to my leg, where sure enough, a

wide ladder had appeared down the back of my thigh. Perfect.

"Jeanne—"

Another song started, the bass so intense that the bathroom door began to rattle. Jeanne headed out.

"Look, if you want to go, just go."

*If you want to go, just go.*

This was ridiculous. She meant go back to Ashley's. I think she also knew that that wasn't where I'd go if I left.

And really, how was I supposed to get anywhere at this time of night? Walk around suburban London in my miniskirt and ripped tights, in an unfamiliar neighborhood? I'd never dream of letting Jeanne do that, especially if I suspected she was upset. But in reverse . . .

I sucked in a deep breath. I shouldn't have come here. I should have made a point earlier.

So, I would just have to do it now.

*Unfamiliar neighborhood, here I come.*

---

It occurred to me that introverts were perhaps among the most discriminated against groups in the world. Starting in primary school, kids were praised for being leaders and always having their hand up in class, for having lots of friends and being able to speak well in front of others. People who preached confidence were considered inspirational, and the kids that were able to follow through were considered role models. Growing up, most jobs required an outgoing personality, and those who weren't like that were regarded as dull or meek. It never occurred to those who thrived in the spotlight that perhaps we introverted people had dreams and desires just as vivid as theirs, that perhaps we were also equally valuable, but in different ways; they'd been taught from the start that their way was the only right way. That our way was a flaw that needed fixing.

That was the problem between me and Jeanne. She

genuinely felt she was doing me a favor by forcing me to do all these things; she didn't realize that I simply didn't want to change. I admired Jeanne, but at the end of the day, I wanted to be myself rather than her. And heck, even she wanted to change.

For blocks, I fought the little voice inside my head egging me to go back. I was more than a bit disappointed that I wouldn't make it to Stonehenge, but a point was a point and it had to be proven.

*And really,* the reasonable part of me said, *do you want to spend the next few days awkwardly crammed together with Chris?*

Nope. No, I did not.

I found a bus station outside the perimeter of a housing estate, a sprawling landscape of hundreds upon hundreds of identical homes in varying states of neglect. The sky here was nowhere near as dark as it had been in Suffolk, polluted by enough light that I couldn't even see the stars.

An old man came to sit beside me, confirming that

this bus would take me as far east as I needed to go. However, it was running late.

When the bus did arrive, it was just as unremarkable as the rest of the surrounding area. I dragged myself to my feet, shuffled after the old man, and took in all the empty seats; there were only three other passengers.

"Excuse me."

"Huh?"

The bus driver was an obese woman with stains of ketchup (at least, I hoped it was ketchup) all over her chest. "I'm not your mother. You have to pay."

I reached into my skirt pocket and felt my stomach drop. I had nothing but a Murray Mint wrapper. My purse and all my money was in my purse back at the flat. I'd used my spare change to get into the club, and there was nothing left.

So, as though the day couldn't get any more mortifying, I was forced to step off the bus and watch it disappear around the corner.

*Well . . . shoot.*

It had been at least a twenty-minute drive from the flat, and I had little to no idea what direction to head in. I considered phoning my mum, then remembered I had no money. I considered going back to Jeanne.

*No. Do* not *do that.*

At least walking around wasn't as bad as I'd thought. There were a lot of odd people hanging around, but nobody really paid me much more than a sideways glance. I kept to the main roads, avoiding alleys like the plague, and tried to remember the way through a haze of churning, unpleasant emotions. Left at the secondhand car dealership, turn right past the school, right again at the brand-new-but-already-looks-dated strip mall . . . and hey, voila, there it was. The nondescript condominium I just about remembered from before.

I retraced my steps to the flat in zombie-mode, ringing the bell to be buzzed inside, praying I wasn't mistaken.

"Hello?"

"Um . . . " I struggled to remember her name.

"Ashley? It's Teresa—Tree—Jeanne's friend. I need to grab my purse."

"Oh." There was a pause. "I'll let you in, hang on."

Ashley helped me scour her flat for my purse, to no avail. To my dismay, it became apparent that if my purse was anywhere, it was still in the car. I hadn't thought about that. If I wanted to go home tonight, I'd have to confront Jeanne again and risk being talked out of leaving.

"Sorry," Ashley said after we'd officially given up. "I can lend you a fiver if you're desperate? I know Jeanne can be a bit, ah, insufferable sometimes."

"Tell me about it," I sighed. "I don't know how I'll be able to pay you back, though."

Ashley shrugged. "I'll take it from your purse later."

Somehow, that wasn't comforting.

I flopped down on her sofa, debating what to do, when the phone started ringing. Ashley waded through a sea of clutter, throwing books and clothes out of the way before finally finding what she was looking for: a vintage 1950's phone.

"Yup?" She glanced at me. "Yeah, she's here. You nearly missed her." Putting one hand over the receiver, she whispered, "Do you want to talk to them?"

*I kind of have to, now you've said I'm here.*

I mentally prepared myself for Jeanne going on about how awesome the club was and how I most definitely could have stayed, et cetera, et cetera. "Yes?"

"Teresa?"

It was Chris, not Jeanne at all. He sounded upset. Maybe he was just slurring.

"Thank god, you didn't . . . " There was enough of a hesitation that I began to think he'd hung up. "We need you."

"Oh?"

I heard him swallow. "There's been an accident."

# Chapter Seven

AN ACCIDENT.

My first thought: *I warned you, Jeanne! Did I not literally just warn you?*

My second thought: *Oh god. Someone's dead.*

"Teresa? Are you still there?"

The hand gripping the receiver was shaking. It didn't feel like mine. I nodded as though he'd be able to see through the wires.

"Wait, hang on, there's . . . Look, we're, uh . . . we're in Colne Valley Regional Park. It's like half an hour away. I gotta . . . "

With a bleep, the line went dead.

"What is it?" asked Ashley, anxiously. "Was that the American boy?"

I nodded again. "I don't suppose you could give me a lift to Colne Valley? I think they're in trouble."

Ashley blinked. "You do realize that park is around twenty-eight thousand acres, right? How the hell did they get out there?"

Because Jeanne probably decided to try avoiding the motorway again, took several horribly wrong turns, and nobody was sober enough to tell her otherwise. It was almost impressive that despite being on the outskirts of London, one of the largest cities in the world, she had still managed to get lost in the middle of nowhere.

Ashley confessed she was nursing a sprained ankle, and with some reluctance agreed to lend me her car in order to track them down. It was an ugly, boxy thing that looked like it had been made out of children's blocks then wrapped in tinfoil, but it would do the job.

As Ashley explained before I left, there were two

major roads running through the park from this direction: one in the northwest and one in the southeast, scaling either side of a series of reservoirs. They converged halfway down the length of the park to form a single motorway, a point that would take the average driver no more than half an hour to reach at night. So, unless Jeanne had started down another minor lane, I'd be able to find them by driving a loop around the northern half of the park. Besides, if Chris was able to locate a phone, then he couldn't have been too far from civilization.

It was a perfect recipe for disaster. Start with a base of midnight and add an absence of streetlights in a regional park, stir well, then beat together a crappy old car and a terrible driver who's suffering major anxiety. Top with the possibility of casualties and bake for half an hour until it looks like a total catastrophe. Voila. Road trip à la Jeanne.

Typical of England, it wasn't a particularly wild stretch of land. I drove past a section of dense forest that quickly bled out into open countryside, straining to see what lay beyond the glare of my headlights. Anywhere Chris may have found a payphone. All that happened earlier was pushed clear out of my mind, overtaken by a single objective: find them.

I came upon a small hamlet near one of the reservoirs just as the clock ticked past midnight. A few minutes later, I spotted Chris sitting on the curbside with his head in his hands. Taking a deep breath, I pulled up beside him and got out.

"Teresa?" He glanced upward, eyes holding such immense relief that it took all my self-restraint not to reach out and hug him. "You found me."

"What happened? Where are the others?"

His head fell back into his hands. His bleached hair was messy, a dramatic change from earlier, and I noticed a deep cut tracing its way across his temple. "We didn't . . . I should've made sure Jeanne was . . . but . . . I wasn't paying attention, and she took the corner so fast I . . . "

"Is she okay?" I scanned the streets for the phone. "Have you called for an ambulance yet?"

He shook his head, wincing as he did so. "Nah. She told me to get you, that you'd know what to do."

So she was all right. My heart hardened.

"Where are you going?" Chris cried, jumping to his feet as I got into the car again. He was more than a little unsteady.

"Get in," I said, "and tell me where to go."

– – –

Sure enough, Jeanne had managed to squeeze down one of the tiniest, most rural lanes the park had to offer. Only this time, she'd succeeded in doing a lot more than simply getting the tires stuck. Skid marks illustrated the haphazard route the car had taken around a corner before piling into a centuries-old oak tree, crumpling the bonnet, shattering the front window, and severely denting the passenger door.

I came to a screeching halt behind the wreckage, leaving the headlights on as I ran over. Chris stumbled after.

"What the ever-loving *heck,* Jeanne?" I gestured to the wreckage, surprised by how angry I was, now the fear had worn off. "How fast were you going?"

Jeanne was sobbing too heavily to be coherent. Her eyes were rimmed in thick liner that was now dripping down her cheeks, her skin red and blotchy. It wasn't a pretty sight.

"In her defense, it was far too dark to see the speed limit," Ritchie said. Like Chris, his words were much fuzzier than they should have been. His dark eyes were unfocused, and there was the faint stench of vomit hovering about him. "And we only had one, two, maybe three—"

"Quiet," I snapped. *Gotta take charge, gotta keep it together* . . . "First things first, is anyone badly hurt?"

Chris shook his head. Ritchie, I noticed, had a nasty bruise materializing under his eye where his head must've slammed into the dashboard, but apart from that, looked fine. He'd been lucky. With Jeanne it was harder to tell.

"Well?" I demanded, trying to keep my tone authoritative. "Are you okay?"

"Um . . . " She sniffled and hiccupped at the same time. "My hand hurts. But not really. Kinda like a headache in my wrist, y'know? Maybe it does hurt." Then she relapsed into tears. "Oh god, Tree, I'm so, so, so sorry. I'm such an idiot."

"Yup," I agreed. "You are."

Very quickly, I established three things:

A mechanic would be ridiculously expensive.

If we decided to get the car fixed, we wouldn't make it in time for the solstice tomorrow.

Chris, thank goodness, didn't appear to have had quite so many drinks as the other two.

"Can you make it go again?" I asked him, realizing how outlandish a request it was. There wasn't even a windshield left to salvage. "I know you're more of an airplane mechanic, but surely you could do something, anything?"

Chris was pale in the headlights, eyes flickering between me and the car. "Teresa . . . um . . . "

"We can buy a new window if we have to, but we can't . . . I can't think of anything else to do," I said, one step away from begging. It had all happened rather quickly, and panic was beginning to set in again.

Ritchie broke the silence with a snort. "He couldn't put Velcro straps together, let alone fix a bloody car."

"Ritchie—" Chris warned.

"Oh, right," Ritchie snorted again. "It's a secret. Sorry. We're strong, capable—"

Chris slapped him.

"What's a secret?" I frowned.

"Nothing. He's not thinking straight."

"Yes, I am!" Ritchie protested.

"Chris—"

"Teresa—"

"Morris!" Jeanne shrieked in anguish, as though realizing what happened for the first time. "You have to fix it, you have to!"

"I can't!" Chris shouted. Everyone fell silent. Then, softer, "Ritchie's right. I can't."

"What do you mean?"

"He means, he's a potato peeler."

"Shut *up*, Ritchie." Chris was pacing, blood smeared across his hands from where he'd wiped the gash on his forehead. "Look, what he's trying to say is that we're not exactly . . . well . . . "

"Not exactly *what?*"

"Fighter pilots." He swallowed. "I work part-time in the mess kitchen doing food preparation. Ritchie's more into, uh, janitorial work. My dad is a squadron leader, Ritchie's dad's a flight lieutenant. We came with them because we'd done nothing with our lives in America and didn't have the money to support ourselves out there."

Everything slowed down. The dust particles dancing through the headlight beams, the moon's progression from behind the branches of the oak, Jeanne's pathetic hiccupping. Stopped.

I gave a shaky laugh. "That's funny."

"This time I'm really not joking."

"So you never really flew for the Queen?"

"I don't even know how to fly."

"And Live Aid?"

"Watched it on TV."

"Spying on the Russians?"

"Nada."

"Having the fastest bike in Mildenhall?"

"That," Chris said, "is actually true. Ritchie's nuts."

Richie nodded in agreement, falling over after attempting to stand up. There was a rip in his leather jacket, exposing his pale arm.

Well then. Part of me was flattered, knowing they made all that up to impress us, but the more dominant part was all the more irritated. My only hope for somehow salvaging this mess of a road trip had been their mechanical expertise, but if that was nothing but a pile of lies, then we were well and truly stuffed. We'd have to pool our money for a tow truck and watch the solstice from some crummy London suburb.

"Tree?"

I glanced over at Jeanne. She truly did look

pathetic, her makeup smeared all over her face and her swollen wrist hanging limply by her side. "What?"

"I really am sorry," she whispered.

"It's your car," I said, trying to sound nonchalant. "Not mine."

Her lower lip quivered. "I felt terrible . . . when I realized you'd really left . . . I didn't think you . . . I thought maybe . . . "

"Are you saying it's my fault that you were going so fast?"

"Yes," said Ritchie.

"No," said Jeanne. "No, I'm glad you didn't go home. That's all."

I opened my mouth to tell her that I nearly had, when I remembered the reason why I hadn't. However, if my purse was in the car, then I'd have more than enough for a bus fare to Stonehenge.

"How much money do you have? All of you?" I probed, automatically reaching for my pockets.

Jeanne started crying because she didn't remember.

Ritchie shrugged and said, seriously, "About eleven-teen dollars."

"Twenty pounds maybe? Give or take?" Chris searched through a wallet tucked in his butt pocket. "Plus my credit card, which has a bit more. Ritchie has about the same."

My head was spinning. Maybe, just maybe, we could bus it to Stonehenge in time for sundown tomorrow. Of course, we'd never make it all the way back home again afterward, but we could cross that bridge when we came to it. As for the car . . . I wondered if it was illegal to leave it where it was. Jeanne's family was well-off; they'd pay any resulting fines without problem.

I relayed this to Chris, who seemed too relieved about my not biting his head off after his revelation to be too concerned about practicality.

"And I can phone my buddy and get him to bring the bikes down! We can motorcycle home!"

"We?" My stomach gave a little twist.

"Sure." He glanced at me slyly. "Why? Afraid?"

I gestured to the wreck, and at Ritchie, who was retching behind the oak. "You haven't exactly inspired me with confidence."

"Fair enough."

I cracked a smile, then sighed. "I think I'll need your help getting these two into the car. And to make sure Ritchie doesn't . . . uh . . . on Ashley's seats."

Chris grimaced. "I'll take it as penance. I deserve it."

I tossed him the keys and ordered Jeanne to get in the passenger side, fumbling through the darkness in an attempt to retrieve my purse from the wreck. The driver's door, despite being relatively undamaged, was stuck fast.

"Darn," I cursed, giving it a series of desperate tugs. "The lock's jammed."

"Is it unlocked?" Chris asked. He was trying to force Ritchie inside the car in the same manner that a cop might treat an uncooperative criminal.

"Course." I jangled the keys to prove it.

Chris abandoned Ritchie for the moment, coming

over to stand directly behind me. I felt my back straighten.

"Let me have a go." After a few tugs, he let go, cursing. "I think it really is locked."

"Told you." Then I sighed heavily. This wasn't a first-time occurrence by a long shot, but unfortunately, the solution never got any easier. I was only glad the windows had been left open.

"What are you doing?" Chris asked, alarmed, as I squeezed my torso through the only-just-torso-sized crack left open by the window.

"What does it look like?" I grunted over the sound of Jeanne apologizing profusely from Ashley's car. "Can you give me a boost?"

"You'll shatter the glass!"

"Gee, thanks." I indulged in an eye roll. "I'm trying to reach the handle so I can wind the window the rest of the way down. *Then* I'll go all the way in."

Chris just nodded. Gave me a boost. Stepped back and watched as I (very ungracefully, it must be said) reached for the handle, wound down the window, and hauled myself into the driver's seat.

Inside, it stunk of liquor and burnt rubber. It was also pitch black, making my search for my purse a long and tedious one. Then, getting out, I remembered our suitcases. Getting them on the bus—and, later, on a motorbike—would be darn near impossible.

"Jeanne?"

"I wouldn't," Ritchie advised, wisely. "She's having a bit of a crisis."

I turned to Chris. "Suitcases?"

"I don't have anything."

"Yeah, but you're a guy. It matters less for you."

He flashed a grim smile, and for the first time since I'd pulled up, I noticed how out of sorts he looked. If anything, I was relieved on his behalf that he wasn't totally sober. It made the fact that he allowed Jeanne to drive a bit more excusable.

"All right," I said, getting into Ashley's car and tuning out Jeanne's weeping. "Let's go."

The headlights swung around, plunging the Morris

into complete blackness, and then we were gone. Nobody spoke again.

# Chapter Eight

WE FOUND OURSELVES IN A HUDDLE ON ASHLEY'S floor the next morning, surrounded by Ashley's junk. Various groans and moans accompanied each of us as we woke up one by one, and aside from that, nothing more was exchanged. What was there to say?

I sat there, sandwiched between a stack of records and an overflowing laundry basket, watching them. To say Ritchie was embarrassed would have been like saying the North Pole got a tad chilly in the winter. He locked himself in the toilet seconds after waking up, pale-faced and drawn, shrugging on his leather jacket in attempt to regain some of his coolness. Chris sat across from me, fixing himself a bowl of Cheerios and avoiding eye contact. As for Jeanne . . . you'd have thought she'd butchered my cat and only just realized it was wrong.

She sat beside me, but far too carefully. Like I was some strict grandparent who insisted upon proper posture. Every now and then I felt her eyes scan the side of my face. She, like the others, said nothing.

*You could have killed someone. You could have killed yourself, and the boys. And for what? What would you have done if I hadn't been around to save you? You're an idiot, a bloody idiot. Don't ever do that to me again. I was scared for you.*

But I wasn't much better, because all I did was eat my cereal too.

We counted and collected bus money. Then we thanked Ashley, and thanked her again much more profusely after she volunteered to have the car towed as an IOU. Ritchie downed several liters of water and a handful of Tylenol. We marched out into the blinding mid-morning sunshine, found the bus stop, and waited.

It occurred to me that perhaps the smartest thing to do would've been to go home. I wasn't a believer in fate, yet it seemed like maybe we just weren't *meant* to finish this journey. Everyone was tired, the tension was suffocating, and after last night, a good portion of good humor seemed to have leaked away from the group. At the same time, the mess only made me more determined to finish what we'd started. And if I was being honest with myself, I *wanted* to see the magic and otherworldliness that Jeanne described at Stonehenge. I wanted to see if she was right, I wanted to say I'd experienced it, and I didn't want to quit when we were so very close. I knew that I'd never get this close again, and I didn't want Jeanne's bad decisions to take this chance away from me. *Oh, sure, we nearly saw the solstice at Stonehenge. No, can't tell you what it was like; my friend was an idiot, so we all went home again. I'm sure it was great, though.*

"Well," Chris said, unable to bear the tense silence

any longer. "Happy solstice, everyone. Blessed be or whatever you're supposed to say."

"Do you think we'll make it?" Jeanne croaked. Her voice sounded unused, unnatural.

I waited for anyone else to respond. "Hopefully."

"Okay."

When the bus came, it was far busier than it had been yesterday evening. Within, there were people standing up and hanging for dear life, forced to get uncomfortably intimate with everyone else around them.

"Where you headed?" the driver asked, noticing our hesitation. When we told him, he said, "Y'know, given where you are, it'd probably be quicker to take the train. The station's on my route."

So that was what we did. Thank goodness Jeanne also had her credit cards with her, loaded with more money than the other three of us combined, and offered to pay whatever we couldn't.

"Does it count as a road trip if we're taking the

train? More of a rail trip, you'd think," Chris said. We all ignored him. He didn't speak again.

It was three hours to Grateley, the closest station to Stonehenge. There would be one stop to change lines, but at least we'd make it in time. Even if we had to walk the rest of the way once we arrived in Grateley, we'd make it in time.

The interior of the train was composed of bright blue velour seats, a beige linoleum floor, and advertisements lining the ceiling next to harsh, white strip-lighting. I sat by the grubby window, turning away as Jeanne sat next to me, with the boys facing us in the other direction. There was an old woman behind me who kept coughing and enough middle-aged men in suits to populate Castle Acre several times. A conductor checked our tickets, robotically enough that I doubted he'd notice if they were dated from years ago, and then we were left to abandon ourselves to the rhythmic chugging of the train as it sped from the station. Skyscrapers and billboards, tangled messes of powerlines, and frequent stops outside of identical stations where people got off to be replaced by doppelgängers in exactly the same suit with exactly the same haircut. Despite being surrounded by people, I was alarmed by how lonely the city felt compared to home.

Unfortunately, our stop required a significant diversion south through the heart of London, where tourists joined the throngs of businessmen and gathered at the windows as we caught a glimpse of Tower Bridge. Chris stood up to let a heavily pregnant woman sit down, and Jeanne was forced closer to me when a particularly . . . *well-insulated* figure took a standing position right beside her.

We were off at Clapham Junction, a station so bustling it was claustrophobic. We all purchased the biggest ploughman's sandwiches I'd ever seen from a kiosk, resulting in us nearly missing our connection as we struggled to finish them. Then we were straight back on a smaller, but otherwise similar train for the long haul.

As we moved farther west, the London commuters

thinned out and the stops became less frequent. Skyscrapers shrunk into more housing estates, and every now and then, it was possible to see the suggestion of greenery.

"Well," Chris said so suddenly we all flinched, "because I never actually went to Land's End, this is the farthest west I've ever gone in England."

"I suppose I win at that game." Jeanne offered a small smile, then retracted it after I remained straight-faced. "You know. Being Welsh and all."

A few minutes of more tense silence, then, "Once, at the mess, we served a meal that was entirely pink."

Jeanne, Ritchie, and I gaped at him with clear what-drugs-are-you-on expressions. He laughed, and it was warm and genuine.

"Seriously. Not quite as fantastic as flying my own fighter jet, but still pretty funny." Chris slipped on his Ray-Bans as we pitched into direct sunlight, continuing, "My boss came in with this massive bottle of pink coloring and just started pouring it into everything. The bread rolls, the gravy, the vegetables—we even painted it over the meat. So I helped serve the officers in the mess—the guys who actually do stuff—and you could see the question marks hovering over their heads. Because everything's *pink*. Then they tuck in and start eating like nothing's out of the ordinary, and I swear, it was the coolest reaction I've ever seen."

On its own accord, my lips curled at the corners.

"And, Ritchie, remember when they did the general survey?" Ritchie gave a slight incline of his head, mouth twitching, and Chris went on, "Well, us Americans are usually decent church-going folk, but word got round that a lot of us younger delinquents were going to write 'Jedi' under religion, because what else were we supposed to write, and sure enough, Mildenhall had to seriously consider hiring twelve Jedi priests based on our response."

"It's a shame they never went through with it," Ritchie mused. "I was considering getting ordained."

At this, Jeanne let loose a muffled guffaw.

"Then there was that time when they posted . . . " Chris broke off, starting to chuckle to himself. "Sorry, they posted joke signs all over base about some escaped moose that had hijacked an incoming plane from Canada, and whenever they were taken down, they'd just reappear again. Warning people not to get too close and all that. So Ritchie and I decide to put together this stupid costume and parade about as this *moose*—"

"Ritchie did that?" Jeanne asked, no longer bothering to stifle her giggles.

"Yeah," Chris said over another bout of laughter. "He made a beautiful moose's butt."

Ritchie made a face that was midway between a scowl, a smile, and a grimace.

"But thing is, we weren't the only ones. The people who were behind the posters also dressed up, so for about two weeks, Mildenhall had two fake moose strutting around base until we ran into each other and realized what was happening. People took pictures and . . . " He shook his head, wiping away a tear. "God, it was so funny. You had to be there. The Great Moose Blight of '86."

I realized I was snickering, my body shaking with repressed laughter. I hadn't even realized it. It was so silly, so outlandish, and I shouldn't have let myself slip because I still had every reason to be angry and yet . . . gosh, it felt like the best medicine in the world. Watching the drab urban scenery transform into lush farmland greener than anything we had in Norfolk, the four of us laughing as though nothing terrible had ever happened . . . the world was once again perfect. If only for a moment.

"I guess truth really is stranger than fiction," I said. "Did you ever do actual work? Any of you?"

"Sure. But there was always a good bit of fun to balance it out. The commanding officers had their hands full." Chris removed his sunglasses and looked at me, piercing blue eyes boring into my hazel ones. "Teresa . . . "

" . . . we're sorry," Ritchie finished.

"Thank you for laughing," added Chris.

"I feel really, really, really guilty." Jeanne sighed.

"It was particularly stupid, even by my standards, and that's saying something."

"She's right. And ditto."

"Seriously, Tree . . . I don't . . . I don't think I'll ever be able to make that up to you, and I'm sorry about not listening to you earlier and telling you to leave and . . . " Jeanne's voice was starting to break. " . . . You're so special to me and I hate to think that I ever gave the impression of not caring enough."

I opened my mouth and closed it several times, unable to squeeze any words between their fragmented apologies, not sure if I should tell them it was okay or not. Jeanne had driven drunk, which could have ended *much* worse, and nearly ruined our entire trip by wrecking the car, not caring if I had decided to go home or not. Plus, there was that whole kissing business . . . yet I was rubbish at holding grudges.

"Well," I said when they finally shut up, "thanks for making me laugh, Chris. And for the apology, all of you. I—"

Jeanne threw her arms around me, so tightly my

breath caught in my throat, and didn't let go. There were no so-mushy-they're-sarcastic professions of our friendship or further requests for forgiveness. Just the hug.

Another set of arms joined in. Then, somewhat awkwardly, came Ritche with wafts of mint, leather, and a fair amount of lingering alcohol.

"This is the part," Jeanne whispered, "that you two say you're sorry for lying to us. And re-apologize for Elm House."

"But that was hilarious."

"Dang it, Ritchie, we're trying to get them to like us again."

We broke apart as the train screeched into another station, where only one person got on and only two got off. The new person gave us a sideways frown, taking the seat farthest away.

"By the way," Jeanne said almost conversationally as the boys returned to their own seats, "while we're being honest here"—was she going to admit her fling with Ritchie?—"I think my wrist is broken. Actually, come to think of it, I probably shouldn't have done the whole hugging thing."

It took a moment or two to register that. Then I realized how pale she was, and how, hidden under the pink and yellow taffeta of her skirt, her wrist was taking on the same shape as a potato and the same color as the skirt.

"Is that from last night?" I exclaimed. "Jeanne, why on earth didn't you say anything?"

"A: far too out of it, and B: didn't want to further hinder the trip." She winced. "Sorry."

Just like that, reality came galumphing back into the picture. Even if one of the few remaining stops had a hospital nearby, getting Jeanne's wrist examined and casted would put a several-hour delay on the journey. Perhaps they'd even ask her to come back the next day, or ask too many questions.

"Can you move your fingers?" asked Ritchie. His expression returned to his usual poker face, but I noticed an unfamiliar concern lurking just below the surface.

"Yeah, but it hurts like hell." She demonstrated, weakly flexing her thumb and index finger.

"Can I see?"

I stood up so Ritchie could come beside her, nearly falling onto Chris as the train picked up speed.

"Maintenance staff often got into medical situations," Chris explained to me. "Basic first aid was especially important for them."

I watched as Ritchie's fingers prodded and poked, ever so gently, as he murmured a mixture of instructions and questions to Jeanne. No presence, no pageantry. Just something oddly tender neither of them showed very often.

"It's not broken badly," Ritchie said after a while, pulling away. Jeanne almost appeared disappointed. "I mean, I'm no professional, but I doubt it's more than a fracture. It must've been from the force of crashing so suddenly while she was holding the wheel."

"So, it won't have to be amputated?"

"Possibly," he replied, so seriously I deliberated

whether he wasn't actually joking. "But if we bind it, it may still be saved."

I rifled through my purse. "I've got that scarf I borrowed back in Elm House. Can you use that?"

I waited for the snarky comment from Jeanne, something along the lines of, *So, that's where it went, you thieving brat,* but she only smiled.

Ritchie took it, untangled it, and nodded with approval. "Perfect."

He made a makeshift cast, much more colorful and characteristically Jeanne than anything she could have gotten from a hospital, bound well enough that her forearm was held straight. Afterward, he didn't make any move to take his original seat back.

"Now," he said with a groan, "does anyone have any coffee?"

"Hangover?" Chris asked.

Jeanne and Ritchie both nodded.

"Good."

Two rude gestures.

With the tension of before melted away, Jeanne

clearly felt it appropriate to do something she'd been wanting to do since boarding the train: fall asleep. To be more specific, fall asleep on Ritchie's shoulder. At first he sat awfully upright, like he was afraid of moving and waking her, then gave in and rested his own head on top of hers.

"Want the window?"

"Huh?" I started, jerking myself away from the *Jeanne & Ritchie Show* to face Chris. I'd almost forgotten I was sitting next to him.

"You look tired, that's all, and you probably don't want *my* shoulder."

*Actually . . .*

"Thanks. But I'm fine."

"Fine," Chris echoed. He made it sound as though the word confused him. Then he shrugged and turned away to face the window himself.

— — —

The train snaked its way through the downs, a range

of ancient chalk hills riddled with pastureland and seemingly purposeless monuments. Just as Norfolk, Suffolk, and Essex were all home to flint cottages, the villages here all sported buildings made out of identical, beige-colored Cotswold stone. The sky was far more overcast here; summer hadn't yet arrived in the west.

Jeanne and Ritchie stayed asleep, only fluttering their eyes open on one instance when a gaggle of rowdy schoolchildren walked through our coach. Chris, who I was beginning to suspect thrived off of talking, tried to strike up several conversations with me.

"Are you still angry?"

"No," I said, not sure if I meant it or not.

"You have every reason to be."

"Oh, I know." I stared at my knees, unsure of whether I should make eye contact. It felt odd, being so close to him. When I glanced at Chris, he was also focused on the floor, fidgeting. "At least you're all being super nice to me now, hey?"

"You deserve it." He grinned. "You're my new hero."

"What does that make you, the damsel in distress?"

"If the damsel thought it was a good idea to chug some potions before climbing out of the tower, then yes." The grin widened, and he finally looked right at me. "Hopefully this means it's happily ever after from here on out."

"Depends on the other two princesses, I think," I said, nodding at Jeanne and Ritchie.

"I'll keep them in check from now on, promise. Well, Ritchie, anyway. Jeanne might need someone with more experience."

"Clearly I don't have enough."

"I get that." His gaze flickered to Ritchie, smile thinning. "You wouldn't believe the crap he's dragged me into. Because I talk more, people assume I'm always the instigator, but . . . he doesn't understand what 'no' means. He's irritatingly persuasive, too."

"What kind of crap?" I asked, watching Jeanne and deciding I completely understood what he meant.

"Just stupid stuff." He shuddered and laughed. "Elm House, for example. Lying about who we were. I mean, I'm good at playing the role, but I wish I was more like you. You had the guts to walk out on Jeanne last night. I knew . . . I *knew* what we were doing, I knew it was wrong, but I couldn't . . . I didn't say anything. I can talk for hours on end about nothing, but when it comes to things that are actually important, I'm useless."

*I wish I was more like you.*

He cut off as the train ground to a halt, startling both Jeanne and Ritchie awake again. It took all of us far too long to recognize this stop as our own, but a sign screaming GRATELEY, HANTS confirmed it. We were here.

# Chapter Nine

IT WAS TEN MILES FROM GRATELEY TO STONEHENGE, a distance that would take us at least three hours to walk. By bus however, it would be an easy, breezy fifteen minutes.

Approximately two hundred miles down. Ten to go.

"Where did all these tourists come from?" Jeanne groaned as we boarded a bus bound for Stonehenge, a bus crammed to the brim with every sort of person imaginable. Barely any had local accents.

"I hate to tell you this," I said, "but *we're* tourists."

*Brilliant. I knew I kept you around for a reason. I meant foreign tourists, genius.*

"I suppose so," she replied instead.

I doubted that on any other day of the year Grateley received many visitors. However, being in possession of the closest station to Stonehenge, hours before the solstice, they'd clearly had to make some adjustments. Deciding that the bus was now at capacity, the driver didn't stop until we arrived at what was easily the biggest makeshift carpark I'd ever seen. We were in the middle of the Salisbury Plain, an area characterized by acres of nothing but treeless expanses of grassland. This enabled visitors to completely override the designated parking spaces and pull up wherever they chose.

"Oh my . . . " I sucked in a breath, stunned by the sheer size of the crowd. "How many . . . ?"

"Ten thousand? Twenty thousand?" Chris shrugged, not bothering to hide his own awe. "And that's just a guess."

Judging by Jeanne's reaction, I could tell she'd not

done her research on the popularity of this event. She, more than likely, had been hoping for something a little less touristy. Something where everyone wore their hair long and loose and dressed in patterns, not a swarm of babbling tourists toting cameras bigger than their heads. I, admittedly, was on the same page.

"Well," said Ritchie, tonelessly, "we made it."

*We made it.*

"So, I suppose now we get as close as we can and wait for the sunset?"

"Uh, no." Jeanne shook her head, still gazing at the mass of cars, buses, and people spread over the plain. "We wait for sun*rise*. That's when the sun aligns with the henge and whatnot."

Ritchie pulled a face like he was a child given nothing except underwear for Christmas. "In all my years, I don't think I've ever, ever, ever been awake for a sunrise."

"Today's your lucky day," I murmured. "Or, rather, tomorrow."

"You slept on the train." Chris waved his hand

dismissively. "You'll be fine. C'mon, let's go before the best seats get taken."

Given it was the longest day of the year, the sun was still high in the sky. Without a sliver of shade to be seen, I quickly found myself melting under the glare, the excess of body heat not helping. A few brave volunteers attempted to police incoming traffic by demanding people purchase tickets, but with nothing more than a flimsy rope to maintain order, they were easy to avoid. Since they had at least successfully managed to keep the vehicles far enough away from the monument, we found ourselves in for a decent trek down a footpath with several hundred others. Cows, munching away in a nearby field, observed with dim interest.

"Gosh, Tree, look!" Jeanne gasped, tugging at my sleeve. Then she hastily retracted, muttering, "Sorry."

I was about to tell her that there was no need to apologize when I caught sight of *it*.

Stonehenge was rather like the Eiffel Tower, or the Empire State Building, or the Colosseum, in that I'd seen so many pictures of it that my initial reaction was, "*That's it?*" swiftly replaced by a more excited "*That's it!*" Usually, in all the pictures I had seen, the stones were rising out of a morning mist like megalithic tombstones, eerie and mystical and, most importantly, deserted. Today couldn't have been more opposite. Every car in that sea of a carpark must have had an average load of five people, who were all gathered right here, flooding the monument in the same way ants might cover a discarded apple core. Even from where we were, still half a mile away, I could hear the hum of thousands of voices and languages, along with a strange, irregular drumming.

"The worst part is," Chris said to Ritchie, "I can't see a hotdog stand. What an absolute bloody outrage. In America, there'd be at least a dozen hotdog stands here, maybe with some mini-donuts or ice cream. England is stuck in the Dark Ages."

A group of young people dressed in getups similar to Jeanne shot him a vicious glare as they passed.

"He's joking."

"Thank you, Teresa." His stomach audibly rumbled. "But not entirely."

The closer we got, the more obvious it was that a good chunk of those gathered were not, in fact, tourists. We were overtaken by a barefoot girl wearing a medieval-style dress and what looked suspiciously like a wolf skin, sandals dangling from one hand and a satchel of odd objects in the other. A large group clad entirely in white robes was holding hands in the middle of the circle, chanting, and a man covered in an impressive array of body paint nodded at us like we were old friends. Even Jeanne, it was safe to say, had found herself swimming firmly within the mainstream in comparison.

"What utter chaos." Jeanne inhaled, soaking it all in. "I'm in heaven."

"Do you reckon we'll be able to go right up to the stones?" I asked.

"Unfortunately I left my baton back at base," Chris joked, "but with Ritchie's face, we'll be sure to part the crowd."

"They'll swoon," Ritchie agreed.

"Whatever works, works," Jeanne laughed. "Ah! I can't believe we're *here*!"

We ran the rest of the way, taking a leaf out of the medieval girl's book and abandoning the path. The drumming grew louder and the stone circle disappeared underneath the heads of the crowd, which was oozing with a smell halfway between incense and campfire.

"Elbows out," Chris instructed, plunging in. "Keep up, guys!"

The sensation was so similar to moving underwater that I found myself holding my breath. Bodies mashed into me from all sides, and given my not-so-generous height, it was like being a little lost child in a busy supermarket. A supermarket for the strange.

Jeanne grabbed my arm as I tripped over an abandoned backpack, elbowing a young man trying to paint an intricate symbol on his girlfriend's forehead.

"Watch it!" he hissed in an obvious posh accent.

"Poser," she retorted. Then, to me, "I mean, who

paints the symbol of a Celtic demon on their face? Someone without a clue, that's who."

"Unless they actually are into all that."

She shrugged. "Maybe. Probably not, though."

I wanted to ask her how *she* had a clue, but before I could, she realized she was still touching me and let go, running to join Ritchie and Chris. I followed, albeit slower, and tried to ignore the feeling of being drowned. In sweat, in smoke, in tourists, and believers . . .

Then I was there. Out of nowhere, the crowd in front of me melted away and was replaced by a block of towering stone. I was struck by how ordinary it looked up close, almost like concrete, polka-dotted with lichen and shallow holes. I traced my hand down a curve. Warmed by the sun, by all the hordes of others trying to touch it, and pulsing with more than five thousand years of history. Not nine hundred like the priory and castle. *Five thousand years.* People had been standing exactly where I was standing, touching this weirdly ordinary rock for five thousand years.

And, despite the sweltering heat, that thought was enough to send a procession of chills dancing down my spine.

The moment lasted only a fleeting instant before I was roughly shoved out of the way. Ritchie rejoined me, declaring he'd had enough of crowds to last a lifetime, and we battled our way back into the open to wait for Jeanne and Chris.

As the rays of sunlight became golden and slid toward the western horizon, the eastern sky darkening, we decided to set up camp for the night. "Camp" being a subjective term, as ours consisted of nothing but the tiny square of grass we'd cordoned off as our own and my bag. Most people had blankets and food and even tents, which, as Jeanne ruefully pointed out, we hadn't owned even before the crash. So Chris disappeared into the crowd and returned with a box of homemade sausage rolls and some much-needed water bottles.

"How'd you get these?" Jeanne asked.

"A magician never reveals his secrets."

"These better be *just* sausage rolls." Ritchie took one gingerly.

"Shut up and be grateful for what the breadwinner has brought you. Anyway, I doubt that after all that's happened, it will be a pastry that takes us down."

"I wouldn't be so sure," Jeanne said. "I had a bizarre encounter with a pork pie once."

– – –

Sleep was a distant fantasy. The sun took forever to disappear, and even when it did, the night remained anything but dark. Camera flashes bleached the blackness with the frequency of lightning strikes. Sparklers—somebody must have been selling them, as there was no way so many people thought to pack them—traced fiery circles and symbols before fizzling away to be replaced again and again and again as the night progressed. It was a mess of drums, chanting, whooping, shouting, an atmospherically inappropriate boom box blasting disco music, laughter, a fiddle, what sounded like fireworks, the shrieking of names, a creepy trumpet thing, random loud bangs, whistles, murmurs, and the steady sound of latecomers crunching into the distant carpark.

We lay on our backs, feet pointing the four directions of the compass, heads touching in the middle. We'd chosen a spot sufficiently far away from the Henge, but were still surrounded by other campers a stone's throw away. I felt every lump and knob in the grass digging into my back, my skinny jeans rendering it impossible to get comfortable, yet there was enough going on that I didn't mind. It wasn't like sleep was going to happen.

"Anyone good at constellations?" I asked, squinting through the artificial light to get a better picture of the stars.

"I can find the dippers, but that's about it," Chris yawned. "See, there's one, and there's the other one."

"That's actually the 'head' of Draco, not a dipper," Jeanne corrected, also yawning. "See, you can see his tail stretching all the way down there." She raised her finger and traced a path through the sky, connecting a twisting trail of stars. "And there's Cygnus—shaped like a crucifix—and that really bright star over there is Vega, next to that tiny circle constellation which is Lyra, the harp. Polaris is . . . "

"Wow," Chris said, impressed, after she'd mapped out what must have been the entire sky. "You know your stars."

"Yeah." I felt her shrug. "I wanted to be an astronomer once."

"You did?" I frowned. "I never knew that. Why did you change your mind?"

"Life got in the way, I suppose. I wasn't quite clever enough, wasn't quite motivated enough, et cetera, et cetera." She sighed. "You know how it works, Tree. Village life seems small at first, but it's so contained that after a while, it becomes everything. There is no other world."

"What about you, Teresa? What would you do, given the chance?" asked Chris.

In all honesty, I'd never thought about it. Jeanne

was right; there was never a reason to leave Castle Acre, so nobody did. We all finished school, rarely ever going on to complete higher education, got jobs in the local businesses, and saved up enough to buy a house so our children could repeat the same steps. *Else* just wasn't done.

"I don't know," I said, honestly. "I suppose I'd be here."

"That's a vague answer."

"It's the truth. Given the chance to do anything, I'd like to visit places like here."

"Can you believe she didn't want to come in the beginning?" Jeanne chuckled. "Where would we be without each other, hey?"

"You," I said, "would be dead. Or in jail."

"And you'd live life like a scratched record."

By the stone circle, someone suddenly screamed, followed by a ripple of hearty laughter.

The others piped down after that, lost in their thoughts, and I attempted to find all the constellations Jeanne spoke about. Around two a.m. I realized my extremities had gone completely numb, the cold ground having soaked up all the heat I'd gained earlier on, so I stood up and walked around. Chris noticed and came to join me. We didn't speak the entire time, our eyes flickering over the various odd or mundane activities other campers were doing in anticipation for sunrise, before returning.

I dozed the remaining hours away until I was woken by a cry. It was about quarter to four in the morning, and ever so slightly, the darkness was fading in the east.

Chris rolled over and shook Ritchie—who had somehow managed to achieve proper deep sleep—awake. "It's starting!"

"Don't care," Ritchie mumbled, batting him away.

"Jeanne?" Chris nodded at her. She came over and they both hiked him to his feet, until he was awake enough to realize what was going on.

The way to Stonehenge itself was a minefield of miniature camps, many containing the motionless forms of those who had partied the earlier night hours away. Those who were awake and moving were quiet, hushed by the spectacle beginning in the sky. I couldn't remember the last time I'd watched a full sunrise, if ever.

"I'm freezing," Jeanne muttered, wrapping her arms around her torso and rocking from side to side as we walked. "Everyone's wearing parkas and fleeces!"

"Me too." I exhaled, releasing a faint cloud.

"Don't look at *me,*" said Ritchie, zipping up his jacket. "I need it as much as you guys."

"I wouldn't want it anyway," Jeanne scoffed, "it's ripped."

"You two are adorable," I said with an eye roll, which normally would have earned a shove from Jeanne. Not today, though.

We joined the main pack of people crowded around the stones, close enough to have a good view, although too far away to be able to touch them. In the dark the people all seemed much more normal than they had yesterday, bundled under blankets and rubbing the sleep from tired eyes. Many were even wearing winter hats, though I caught a glimpse of someone wearing antlers nearer the stones. Ah, diversity.

"This is going to take forever. I could've had another hour," Ritchie sighed.

"We'd lose our seats," I pointed out. Already, the space behind us was filling with rows upon rows of onlookers. And, with every passing second, the light in the east grew brighter as the sky shifted from black to navy to a pale blue-gray, strips of ashen clouds replacing the stars.

"This is a really stupid question," Chris said, directed at Jeanne, "but what happens? What's the hullabaloo about?"

"Midsummer's night is a symbol of new beginnings," she explained. "The Celts celebrated it with fire, and many pagans believe it's when magic is strongest in our world, and—"

"But *Stonehenge?*"

"Shut up and watch," I told him, quite mildly. "Then maybe you'll see."

Jeanne grinned at me. I grinned back.

As Ritchie predicted, it took a long time coming. Across the plain, with thousands of impatient eyes looking on, rays of insipid yellow added the first splash of color to the sky. Then pinks and oranges, and finally, the harsh blood-red glow of the sun itself.

A group of kids about our age sat up on each other's shoulders and started throwing glitter around, chanting, "Sol-stice! Sol-stice! Sol-stice!"

Another group, whom I presumed to be the bona fide druids, moved into the middle of the circle and held hands, chanting in a different, beautiful language.

As the shadows receded, the first rays washed over us and dimmed the chill. I was barely aware of how cold it was now; there was too much else to focus on. The atmosphere was one of anticipation, and you could feel it in the energy of the crowd. Nobody seemed to remember what ungodly hour it actually was.

"Whoa," Chris exclaimed. "It's rising right in the middle of—oh! I get it. That's the cool part, isn't it?"

Jeanne nodded. "Yeah. Every year, for millennia, the sun has risen directly between those stones on the solstice."

The stones in question were the more iconic of the circle, the ones that formed square arches by having horizontal slabs on top of them. The sun, inch by inch, rose exactly in the middle of that arch. That meant, if the plain were empty and the circle still complete, there would be a perfect shadow in the west.

"Sol-stice! Sol-stice! Sol-stice!"

I recognized the posh couple from last night in the crowd, symbols still painted on their faces. They had their eyes closed and were moving their lips in perfect synchrony, ignoring everyone else around them.

"Hey," I elbowed Jeanne, "what do you know?"

"I can top that."

She bent down, grabbed a handful of trampled clover, sprinkled it in her hair, raised her arms to the sky, and began singing. Not in Celtic, or even anything relatively close to that. No, she began singing the theme song of a children's television program.

"Oh God," Chris laughed. "Jeanne, no."

"Why *that* song?"

She ignored us, still singing as the sun continued to rise. The people next to her, far from being irritated, laughed too. A few began singing songs, too.

The sun rose higher, the energy in the gathered crowd gained momentum, and the sky grew more and more spectacular. In a gesture of unspoken unity, everyone raised their hands and stretched their fingers open wide, capturing the sun from ten thousand angles. It was cheesy and magical and intensely personal at the same time, the sort of *other* feeling that had to be experienced to be understood.

"Sol-stice! Sol-stice! Sol-stice!"

Chris had a Cheshire cat grin plastered across his face, Ray-Bans in place and reflecting the stone arch. Ritchie was also participating, tattered jacket hanging off his arms, eyes glazed over as though contemplating a particularly deep thought, which he probably was. Jeanne had her eyes closed and was smiling a very contented smile. She looked at home.

Well, on second thought, *everyone* looked at home. The girl with dreadlocks down to her ankles and the middle-aged woman wearing a sensible overcoat, the obvious tourists with their cameras flashing madly, and those here for a more spiritual purpose . . . there simply wasn't such thing as a poser. Because all these people came and were here, and as the sun peaked over Stonehenge, nothing else held any consequence. Jeanne was the real deal, and so was I, and so was the rest of the crowd. We were all watching the same sunrise, no matter why we were here or where we came from or who we were. Nobody set rules dictating when we were "in" enough to belong. It was special for all of us.

We let out a cheer when the sun finally cleared the arch. The hush lifted and people began to chatter and shout and sing again, some even hurrying back to their camp in order to catch a few extra winks.

"For something very ordinary, that was very cool," Chris said, still grinning.

Jeanne, hands and head thrown back, did a

pirouette. "Ah, my life is now complete. Seriously. I can die happy."

"Good," I chuckled, "because our only way home is on their motorcycles."

Ritchie's eyes widened. "Oh, no."

Chris clapped him on the shoulder. "Feeling sufficiently sober, old buddy?"

"If you call me that again, then I'll have sufficient reason not to be." He cracked the ghost of a smile, aimed at Jeanne. "Give me a few hours. It'll be fine."

"Knowing Jim, it'll be more than a few hours. He's the one towing them over," Chris added. "He owes us several significant favors."

The crowd began dispersing, some to their cars in an effort to beat the rush, many to pockets of other festivities striking up, and more shifting to try and get a better view of the sunrise. We stayed where we were, shoulder to shoulder, squinting—with the exception of Chris and his Ray-Bans—at the eastern horizon. Jeanne tilted her head sideways to rest it on Ritchie's shoulder. He tensed, glancing at Chris and I for a reaction, and when we pretended not to notice, he slipped his arm around her waist.

*Kissing behind a public toilet is totally fine, but PDA in front of best friends is making you nervous? Ha.*

Soaking it all in as much as possible, I wondered what would happen when it was all over. If Jeanne would chalk Ritchie down to a fleeting summer fling or make an effort to continue seeing him. If I would ever keep in touch with Chris.

"Happy solstice!" An androgynous figure wearing what could only be described as an ornate Halloween costume (with bells, bright face paint, and a strange, tattered overcoat) danced past, handing both Jeanne and I dead flowers.

"Yes," I said, unable to think of anything else to say. "It is."

# Chapter Ten

*I*DIDN'T REALIZE HOW DISHEVELED I WAS UNTIL I SAW my reflection in the mirror of a gas station bathroom. My hair, usually moussed and curled, hung limp around my shoulders. My makeup was gone altogether, and my clothes were rumpled and covered with grass stains. I'd have killed for a shower.

"*Au natural,*" Jeanne said, appearing from a stall and shuddering at her own reflection.

"Mm. Artfully scruffy."

"That's it." She whipped a tube of bright red lipstick out of a hidden pocket in her skirt, pouting and applying. "Want some?"

"No, thanks. I'm embracing my descent into total disarray."

"How very dignified of you, Tree," she said in a false English accent. She leaned forward and kissed the mirror, leaving a perfect imprint of her lips on the glass, before exiting. She didn't wait for me; I think she was making an effort to give me space, or independence, or something.

I hovered a few minutes more. Stonehenge already felt like worlds away, even though we'd only left about an hour ago. Jim-with-the-trailer showed up around midday and, fed up of the crowds by then (and desperately needing a toilet break) we'd left straightaway for Amesbury, the nearest village. We didn't yet know exactly how we were getting home, and a part of me wanted to take as long as possible. Maybe dip into Jeanne's home country of Wales, which was only a few hours northwest, or turn Chris's lie of biking to the furthermost tip of Cornwall into a reality, only a few hours southwest. Then, the more rational part of me realized how terrifying that would be via motorbike.

Jeanne, obviously, saddled herself with Ritchie, so I was left awkwardly clinging onto Chris for dear life as he hit speeds that the car never would've been able to reach. I was glad I hadn't eaten before we left. At least the sprawling roads of Salisbury Plain involved few bends, but the idea of winding our way through a city—or anywhere that wasn't open countryside—was nauseating.

"I say we follow the same route home," Chris suggested when we reconvened. "We'll stop at Ashely's again to, ah, check up on the car, and then gun it the rest of the way back in one go."

*Then what?* Life went on, I supposed.

"Speaking of gunning it," Jeanne said, "my wrist is killing me. I'm not sure how tightly I'll be able to hang on."

"Oh, crap." Ritchie appeared to have forgotten that little detail.

Jeanne decided, after milking our sympathy for a while, that she would be fine. She demonstrated how she'd use her good hand to clamp onto the other one, making me wonder if it really was broken at all (the swelling had definitely gone down). Then we were off again.

Before, I pictured the boys' bikes to be *Top Gun*-worthy machines, all chrome exhaust pipes and shiny colors. After their revelation, my standards had substantially lowered. In fact, had they produced children's tricycles I doubt I'd have been that surprised. So when Jim unloaded two proper motorcycles, regardless of their condition, I was impressed. Chris's was barely more than a moped, with a front light the size of my head and tiny wheels with spokes that reminded me of a bicycle. It was a rusted cobalt blue, and sported circular wing mirrors that gave the illusion of ears, somehow. Ritchie's was a tad cooler, solid black with a crimson leather seat and the Honda branding still intact, clearly restored—with questionable skill—to make it faster. Both were at least a decade old.

The helmet Chris gave me stunk of sweat and kept slipping down over my eyes. Luckily it had a full visor, so at least I was spared being blinded by the wind on top of everything else. It was an odd feeling, glancing down at my feet and seeing the tarmac rushing mere inches underneath them, and after a while, I'd almost forgotten that the figure I was holding on to was Chris. The seams of my skinny jeans were digging in like crazy, though, and I doubted whether or not I'd ever be able to sit down again. It was far from the romantic situation I'd envisioned.

The green downs and Cotswold stone villages shifted back into a more urban scene as the afternoon drew on, and the journey grew more interesting. We nearly toppled sideways at a set of traffic lights when I, apparently, "distributed my weight wrong." Memories of the solstice sunrise and Stonehenge preoccupied my thoughts enough that I paid next to no attention to the present situation, and even though it took several hours to arrive in London, I barely processed more than a few minutes.

"You're in luck," Ashley told Jeanne. "The mechanic guy said the car is salvageable. It will be around a week, at the very least, before it's running again, however."

She went on to name the horrifically high number that Jeanne owed her for having the car towed, high enough that I wondered if she'd added interest. Jeanne didn't question her.

The night passed much more uneventfully than it had last time we were in London, everyone dead-on-their-feet exhausted. We slept in, woken up at ten a.m. when Ashley's boyfriend arrived to take her to work. I managed to beat the others to the shower, freshening up just in time to become all sweaty and windswept on the back of Chris's motorcycle again. Clearing London was a painfully slow affair, dragged out all the more thanks to Jeanne's injury. As I took it all in, the identical buildings and identical people, how nobody gave you a sideways glance, I decided that even if I did go to school and try for a proper career, I wouldn't come to the city. I'd come home.

"You all right back there, Teresa?" Chris shouted,

weaving in and out of stalled cars along the motorway. "We're nearly out."

I nodded, every part of my body aching and my stomach lurching with each turn. Absolutely peachy.

Fortunately, most morning traffic was heading into London rather than out of it, so we managed to escape within an hour. Enter the suburban towns, networks of council estates and supermarkets and immaculate school playing-fields. On a motorbike, it was faster to weave our way through these than risk getting jammed in an A-road queue.

"Holy roundabouts, Batman," Jeanne called, riding parallel to us now the roads were quieter. "I feel like we're on some fairground ride. I've nearly fallen off, like, twice."

"Three times," Ritchie corrected.

Another roundabout loomed ahead, this one the center of five intersections. It must have been newly built, as the decorative trees in the middle were no more than sticks.

"With that gimpy grip of yours," I said to Jeanne,

"I bet you, say, five pounds that me and Chris can clear that faster than you two."

"Make it ten," Jeanne grinned, brightening at the idea of a bet, "and I reckon we can beat you going around the *wrong way.*"

"Because speeding isn't dangerous enough?" I laughed. Then I realized she wasn't joking.

Chris and Ritchie shared a glance, sizing each other up. A dark, sardonic smile appeared behind Ritchie's visor.

"You really shouldn't have said that," Chris sighed.

"Wait—" I began.

I was cut off by the screeching of engines and tires as both boys shot off, Ritchie narrowly managing to squeeze ahead of us. The roundabout was upon us in less than a heartbeat, and to my utter dismay, they headed straight into the oncoming traffic. I shrieked as a bus bore down on us, honking madly, and another car was forced to swerve off the road to avoid hitting us.

"Stop, stop, stop!"

"Go, go, go!" Jeanne squealed. "We're gonna—argh!"

She must have slipped, as Ritchie slowed down which enabled Chris and I to whiz past.

"Chris!"

Another bus. More honking. Me screaming, Jeanne shrieking for Ritchie to hurry up. Then, just like that, we were stopped on the side of the road, the roundabout behind us.

"Owned," Chris jeered. "High-five, Teresa!"

I tapped his hand weakly.

"Rematch," Ritchie demanded, taking off his helmet and shaking his hair. "Jeanne—"

"Owes me ten pounds," I interrupted, glaring at her, "and an extra twenty for giving me a heart attack."

"Okay," she said, in such a way I knew she'd never dream of paying up. Then she frowned. "Ritchie, you're shaking."

"Must have something to do with staring death in the face," I suggested.

"Nah," Chris chuckled, "he's allergic to losing."

"Well, then you must be allergic to winning, because you have the shakes too," Ritchie snapped. "I suppose it's a shock for you."

It turned out that that little escapade hadn't just freaked *me* out, so we walked the bikes over to a nearby carpark to laugh it off.

Chris exhaled out of the corner of his mouth. "That was actually nuts."

"This entire trip has been nuts." Jeanne adjusted the scarf wrapped around her wrist, kicking at loose gravel and pacing back and forth. "We need to plan to do it again some time."

I thought about Elm House and the tapered lanes, of terrible mistakes and the amazing spectacle of Stonehenge. But even the lowest moments wouldn't stop me from doing it all over again.

"Where would we go?" I asked.

Jeanne thought. "I don't know. Paris? We could cross the channel on one of those hovercraft things."

I wrinkled my nose, the unpleasantness of London

still fresh in my mind. "How about north? Into the Lake District?"

"Or farther," Chris suggested. "Scotland. Loch Ness. The Highlands."

"Even up there I'm sure we'll manage to make stupid memories. There are more stone circles in the north, after all," Jeanne mused. Then, with a guilty glimpse at me, "But of the good kind. Promise."

So, that was that. None of us really believing it would ever happen, we agreed to reconvene next summer to try and push as far north as the roads allowed. Theoretical as it was, there was some comfort in the possibility of this not being the end.

We moved onward. Strange roads became familiar ones. There was the sign welcoming us to Essex, and there was the village with the Crown and Thistle. Then we were in Suffolk, and signs counted down the miles to Mildenhall. Fifteen miles, seven miles, one mile . . .

It was odd. We'd dragged out the journey west for so long, and nothing but petrol stops and traffic had held us up going east. Maybe the bikes felt faster than the old car. Maybe time slowed down when you didn't have a deadline.

We weren't allowed to go in, so the boys pulled up outside the barbed-wire fences to let us off.

"Well," Chris said, awkwardly.

"Well."

"Well."

"Well."

Absently, I did a few squats in effort to regain feeling in my legs. Several planes took off from the runway on the other side of the fence, roaring through the countryside silence, and I noticed the guards at the base gates watching us.

"Thanks for dragging us along." Chris held out a hand for us to shake, then retracted it again. "Um . . ."

"One day," Jeanne interjected, saving him, "we'll scare you as much as you two did to us."

"I don't doubt it," Ritchie drawled.

"No, we will."

"Okay."

"Okay."

"Okay."

We stared at each other. What to say? We'd only known each other a few days. Of course, it felt more like I'd been to the edge of the universe and back with them.

Then Chris announced, what the heck, why didn't they take us the rest of the way back to Castle Acre? It was an hour away by bus, so it seemed silly to abandon us like this. And, he went on, he wanted to see our home village.

This gave us an extra forty minutes to stew over the notion of saying goodbye. For me, it was especially strange; since nobody ever left Castle Acre, I'd never had to say goodbye like this. Of course, there was always the possibility that we actually would meet up again next year, but with people like the boys and Jeanne, I knew better than to bank on it.

Jeanne had obviously been mulling over the same thing, as when we pulled up on the outskirts of the village, she threw her arms around Ritchie before he even had a chance to get off the bike. He stumbled sideways, knocking her arm.

"Oh, I—"

She kissed him, full on the lips, ignoring whatever pain she was in. Ignoring Chris and I, ignoring the stares of the locals peeping through their curtains.

I colored and looked away.

"Well," Chris said, "that makes my offer of a hand-shake look lame."

But he extended a hand anyway.

Then Jeanne, fighting back tears, broke away from Ritchie and ran down the lane into the village. And, me being me, I ran after her. When I looked over my shoulder they were both gone.

Just like that.

# Chapter Eleven

THE SECOND I WALKED INTO MY HOUSE, THE ROAD trip felt like it happened forever ago. The boys, the solstice, all of it. My mum hugged me, apologizing for not telling me about Jeanne's plan, went on about how glad she was I got home safely, then started berating me when she realized I'd left my suitcase in London. I opted not to tell her why.

Jeanne didn't visit me for a few days. When she finally did, her wrist was properly bound in gauze (apparently it was a sprain, not a break), and she was wearing a flower crown similar to what we'd seen at Stonehenge.

"I forgot to get his number!" she wailed, the second I opened the door.

"Whose?"

She stared at me like my eyes had gone black. "Ritchie's."

With a dull thud, I realized I hadn't gotten Chris's either. It was a shame.

Jeanne, I was surprised and pleased to note, began referring to me as Teresa rather than Tree. When I pointed that out, she gave her sincerest apology yet for her actions, and we talked everything out. The world was back to normal again.

Summer dragged on, one of the coldest on record. I kept working at a spa shop, and Jeanne began working as a live-in nanny at a nearby stately home. Come September, reviling the idea of another purposeless year, I made the decision to go to school. It was something that would've terrified me months ago, but if nothing else, that road trip had made me braver. England wasn't quite so big anymore. There was a college in King's Lynn, a town not too far away from

Castle Acre, where I was accepted to study journalism. I'd never had the imagination for stories, but found a penchant for real-life reporting; I was even offered a job by a regional newspaper just before my nineteenth birthday.

"And guess why they wanted me?" I asked Jeanne over the phone. "They liked an essay I wrote on the solstice!"

"Teresa Swanson, you smarty pants," Jeanne laughed. "Gosh, do you feel grown up?"

"Horribly so."

"Hang on. Give me two seconds to get ready, and I can fix that."

"How?"

"Shh."

"Wait, wait; do I need to pack?" But the line went dead.

Jeanne still dragged me into stupid situations, but kept them firmly inside the line of the law now. I tried to convince her to come to college with me, or even try for university so she could actually study astronomy, but she never went through with it. She quit being a nanny, hating her boss, and moved in with another family to take care of their disabled daughter. Then she quit that to become a waitress, citing better pay, then decided she didn't need a job at all. Her parents clearly thought differently, since by the time June rolled around again, she'd joined a private Montessori school as a teaching assistant.

"I quite like teaching," she told me. "I'm thinking of going abroad to teach English for a few years. Maybe France, or Italy, or Switzerland. Mum said she had a friend who taught in Argentina for six months—how awesome would that be?"

"You can't leave me!" I exclaimed, aghast. "Jeanne, you can't!"

"Shocking," she teased. "Teresa the Independent needs me too." Then she grew serious. "Thing is, I'm kind of getting itchy feet here. I want to travel again, even if it's only to . . . I don't know, Ipswich."

"Don't let anyone hear you say that," I warned with mock seriousness. "They'll lynch you." Ipswich,

Suffolk, was the rival team to Norfolk's Norwich in practically every sporting event.

Joking aside, I understood what she meant. With the solstice of 1988 rapidly approaching, I couldn't help reminiscing about the mystery and starry skies of last year. I almost felt homesick for it. Jeanne probably would've planned another trip by now, except for the fact she was still waiting for the boys to reach out to us first. They knew where we were. Their silence made me wonder if they'd gone back to America.

A week after final exams, I got another call from Jeanne. She sounded scarily excited.

"Meet me at the priory carpark!" she ordered, before I had a chance to even say hello. "And, yes, you need to pack. As much as you can."

"Jeanne . . . "

The lined clicked and died.

That was when I began to wonder. I didn't want to get my hopes up, but I hadn't heard Jeanne sound so animated for ages.

Self-consciously, I hauled a little suitcase crammed

with all possible essentials through the winding village lanes to the priory, surrounded by visitors for the summer months. And there, amidst the picnicking families and elderly tour groups, were Chris, Ritchie, and Jeanne, waving at me wildly from a convertible they'd dragged right out of the previous decade.

My jaw dropped.

"Come on, Tree-Tree," Chris said, pushing up his new, nondescript sunglasses so I could see his wink. "We're going to Scotland."

– – –

At *this* stone circle, there are no crowds. The stones are far less majestic, thinner and jagged and spaced far apart. Red heather forms a barrier between the circle, the gray-green plain, and the steely loch beyond. In the distance, on the other shore, clouds are beginning to roll over the hills and signal in the nighttime. The magic here is quieter.

Ritchie and Jeanne stand by the water, talking

softly. Neither of them had found anyone else in their year apart, and from what I can gather, Ritchie is considering applying to stay in England permanently, so Jeanne wants to rekindle whatever relationship started last summer.

Chris, ever unable to stand alone, moves beside me.

"I forgot to compliment your hair," he says, awkwardly.

Ordinarily, I'd roll my eyes at the idea of such small talk in a place like this. But I've been waiting for him to notice, so I blush and thank him. Fed up of the purple and feeling brave, I dyed my whole head brown again, ditched the mousse and adopted feathery layers, and bleached my fringe blond. I'm about ninety percent sure I like the change.

He follows my gaze to Ritchie and Jeanne. "You know, I think they might be all right. They've been better this time around."

"Yeah," I agree. "She's been pining over him all year, so I'm pleased for her."

"Same with Ritchie, though he'd never admit it," Chris chuckles.

It's been a week's journey up to the Orkney Islands, and we might take even longer going back. I hope we do. Already, we've decided to let Jeanne show us Cardiff next summer—if Chris is still here, of course. Unlike Ritchie, he's decided to stay in the Air Force and try his hand at becoming a proper pilot. Unfortunately, that means returning to America. It's a shame, and I can't help obsessing over what might have been, but in truth, I think we were always better off as just friends. At least I've gotten to know the real him; not a too-cool-for-school stereotype, but as someone who, deep down, is just as full of self-doubt as me.

The moon is rising, despite it not being dark yet. There are no cheers to accompany it, only silence, and a chill that's making me glad I brought a jacket this time. It's beautiful all the same, and I wish there were a camera capable of capturing it.

On the shore, Jeanne is dipping her feet in the

water, holding her bunched-up skirts above her knees. Ritchie is standing beside her, as close to smiling as he ever gets. One by one, pinprick stars emerge in the wide, wild sky, and the stones encircling us fade to black silhouettes. The air smells like heather and salt, and with the steady sound of waves lapping the pebbled shoreline, I feel as though I'm in a dream. We're the only souls around for miles, but it's a good kind of lonely.

I take a deep breath and exhale, slowly. Chris copies me. And I think, even with adulthood lurking around the corner and reality remaining its ever-present self, I am happy.

Chris will leave, Jeanne and Ritchie's relationship might pull them both away from me, and maybe, this is the farthest from home I'll ever go.

But now, I am happy. And no matter what happens next, these memories will be mine to hold forever.